A Shackled Shipment

C. Lanette

ISBN: 9798404584608

DEDICATION

I'd like to dedicate my first book to my support system. My family and my best friend/partner have been my emotional and physical support throughout my journey in putting my thoughts and imagination into real life paper books.

Thank you all with much love!

CONTENTS

Chapter 1. *Pow! Pow!*

Knock, knock.

I glanced at my roommate, Stacey Walker, who was closest to the door but hadn't moved. Irritated, I stood up in the most dramatic way possible, but she never looked up from her phone. Before I could touch the door, though, it was kicked open and slammed into the wall. Two men in hoodies swarmed in before I could react. The first guy stopped in front of me, and I watched as one of his arms swung out from behind his back and he pointed a gun in my face.

"Gimme everything in this, bitch."

Looking to my roommate, I saw that she was being confronted by the other gunman. I turned back, swinging my fist at the same time to add momentum to my punch, and landed it on his jaw. Stunned, he stumbled back toward the seventy-five-inch television that Stacey brought home barely a week ago.

As he tried to catch his balance, I glanced at Stacey and saw them tussling too. I pushed my guy as hard as I could, and he fell into the already-leaning television, cracking it down the middle along with the stand it was sitting on. Stacey was on the ground, the gunman throwing punches at her. When I looked back my guy was already back on his feet. He pointed his gun right at my head and pulled the trigger.

Click.

I blinked as I heard the gun jam. The gunman and I exchanged looks of confusion, then my anger took over and I swung at him again. This time, we staggered toward the Christmas tree my girlfriend and I had bought just the night before, that still only had a handful of ornaments. He stumbled and fell into it, breaking branches during his fall.

Worried that the gun might not jam on his next try, I didn't look back to check on Stacey. Instead, while the gunman was still trying to get up, I delivered four or five punches to his face and then wrapped my arms around his neck, hoping to make him pass out.

Pow! Pow!

I let go as I felt the guy's muscles loosen, and we both turned toward the shots as the second gunman screamed, "Let's go! Let's go!"

Before I could gather my thoughts, the guy brushed off me, making me stumble a little. Trying to catch my balance, I walked toward Stacey. She was holding her stomach, and blood was dripping out like a river. I stopped in shock. I'd never sat well with blood. She had her phone in her other hand and was trying to call her boyfriend. She put it on speaker each time, but he never answered.

I ran to the door and made sure they were gone before locking it, even though it wouldn't close completely since being kicked in. I turned back to find

Stacey half-limping, half-crawling toward her room, a trail of blood behind her. As she fumbled to the floor, I ran after her, grabbing towels from the closet. I leaned over her in a panic and put one over the gunshot wound in her ribcage. I had to look away to keep from passing out at the sight of the blood as I put pressure on the wound. She wasn't acting like she was in great pain, but she was always one to act tough, like she couldn't ever show emotions.

Neither of us had thought once to call for real help. I finally yelled at Stacey to call 911 instead of her boyfriend, who still wasn't answering. At first, she stared at me like she'd seen a ghost. Then she handed me the phone, and I dialed 911. I told the operator that there'd been a home invasion, and my roommate was shot, lying on the floor and bleeding out. I heard her call for an ambulance and a police unit to the address I gave her.

As we waited, I cleaned up some of the mess in the living room, where the television and the Christmas tree were scattered in pieces all over the floor. I looked for my phone, but it was lost somewhere under the debris. The coffee table had been flipped over, and the decorations on top of it were now all over the floor and couch. The video game system and games from the TV stand were now lying everywhere, and the boxes full of ornaments for the tree had been crushed by the gunman's body and then thrown around.

I heard cars pull up and ran to the door. I poked my head out to make sure they were just cops or EMTs and then opened it all the way when I saw the red and blue lights. The cops walked in and looked at the mess in the living room, then asked me what happened. As I directed them to the back, where Stacey was lying, I tried to summarize so they could act quickly to find out who'd done this. But they never once asked me about the guys. In response to the short amount of concern they were giving me, I fell silent. Finally I said, "Are you going to ask me anything about the intruders?"

One of the three who were standing near me said that most intruders got away.

I walked away from the room after that and found two other cops searching the living room and throwing things around. Confused, I spun around, trying to take everything in, and another cop came from the back room.

"Are you Mercedes Flint?"

I told him yes as though I was questioning his question. He grabbed my arm and snapped handcuffs around my wrists. He turned me toward the door, walked me out to his squad car, and opened the back door, putting his hand on my head to push me in. I looked up to see my roommate on a stretcher, being wheeled into an ambulance. The EMTs left the door wide open, and Stacey's kittens were looking out after her. Sitting in the police car, I could see my girlfriend's car coming towards the house from up the street.

The officer pulled out before my girlfriend arrived and drove to the station. When we turned into the parking lot, a wave of cold passed through my body like I'd been dropped in a tub of ice water. The officer got out and opened the door. The station was just a plain building with yellowish-white concrete walls, lots of windows I couldn't see through, and a wide, glass door the officer escorted me toward. As it slid open, we walked into a room with a body scanner or X-ray device—I wasn't sure which, but something more complicated than a metal detector. He walked me right past the machine to the next set of doors, which opened when he pressed a small button like a doorbell. Inside, I saw bright walls and half-walls with inmates sitting behind them so you could still see their upper bodies.

The officer walked me in, spoke to another, female officer, and then told me to follow her. She took me into a bathroom with a toilet, a sink, and a gated shower you could see right through. She shut the door tight and stood in front of it as she sifted through a basket full of orange clothes. She handed me a set.

"Take all of your clothes off," she ordered.

I did as I was told.

"Now turn around, hands above your head, squat, and cough."

I squatted and coughed in embarrassment, still shivering from the cold of the building. Then she told me to put the oranges on, and I proceeded to, in disgust. The clothes smelled like mildew and burnt baloney sandwiches. As I pulled the orange pants up to my waist, I noticed holes and random stains on them.

I picked up my own clothes and followed the officer out of the bathroom and through another door to the right, into a sort of locker room. She pointed me to a chair in front of a desk. The woman behind it started typing on her computer and asking me for information.

"What's your full name, address, and date of

birth?"

After I answered, she turned in her chair and grabbed a transparent blue bag with a built-in hanger. She handed it to me. "Put all your belongings in here, and we'll keep it until you're released or transported."

The other officer waved for me to follow her, and we walked out to the next station on the right. There was a computer there, with some screens and pads next to the keyboard. She made me stand across from it, where a pair of footprints were taped on the floor, and told me to face forward, left, and right as she took my picture. I understand now why they call them mugshots, because that's exactly what she got from me.

After that, she made me sit in the half-walled square until she finished processing me in the system. I pulled my arms inside my stiff, orange shirt to keep from shivering. It was already just 59 degrees outside, and the air conditioner was on in here.

Looking around the station, I saw a couple of doors marked "Hold." Only one of them also had the word "Women" on it. I heard voices everywhere, from inmates to officers, all of them seemingly competing to talk the loudest. I overheard one officer say that the cells were over capacity, and that men had to be moved into one of the two women's holding cells.

Clank!

I looked up to see a tiny window open on one of the holding cell doors, and an officer rolled up a phone that looked like it was stolen from a telephone booth. I saw many hands come out of the hole and then heard loud arguing. The window was so small and close to the ground that you could only see faces if you bent over and put your face close. One hand finally came out and pulled the phone through the tiny window.

A sliding glass door opened next to one of the holding cells, and I heard yelling. It sounded like a man hollering at another inmate. An officer walked out to the middle of the floor where the other officers sat at computers and looked down at me. "This one needs to go in a cell?" he said.

"Yes, I'm finishing up the processing now. You can put her in the holding cell," the officer behind him said, handing him a piece of paper. He nodded at me to stand up and walked toward the door that read "Women."

"This is your inmate number. You use it for commissary, phone, and visitation. Don't let anyone take it or see it, or they can steal your commissary and your phone call minutes." He handed me the paper.

When he put the key in, it sounded like thirty or forty locks moved inside the door. There was a loud *pop!* as the pressure was released, and it cracked open. As soon as the door was open wide enough for me to see inside, I found ten or so pairs of eyes focused on me. There were beds on the floor. As I turned back toward the officer, he handed me an orange, canoe-shaped board and a beat-up green mat.

"It's a boat you put on the floor. Place your mat in it, and you have yourself a bed." He smiled.

I grabbed my equipment and walked slowly in. The cell couldn't have been more than ten by ten feet, with a bunk bed on the left and concrete blocks along two walls that were being used as benches. Straight across from the door was a tiny wall that I assumed hid the toilet. The only window was a little square with screens both inside and outside. It looked like someone had put wet tissue paper on it. I guessed they were trying to insulate the room from the cold outdoors. There was only one spot on the floor big enough for my boat, apart from the little space directly in front of the toilet. I set my things down and turned toward the door as it began to close. I was fixing to ask where my blanket and sheets were, but as I glanced across the roomful of eyes still gazing at me, I saw that only two people had blankets. So I just sat down on my mat and grabbed my cold arms. There wasn't room to really do anything besides sit on your mat and use the bathroom.

I noticed a phone on the little wall in front of the toilet. I walked over to it, but someone called out, "It's broke" before I could pick up the receiver.

"What's wrong with it?" I asked.

No one did anything but shrug. I picked the receiver up and heard nothing. I followed the cord to the phone box and found a cut part, with broken wires hanging out like someone had tried to pull the receiver completely off the box. There were papers taped up around the phone with the names and numbers of bail bondmen and lawyers.

I was studying engineering at the time, and my mind went into problem-solving mode. I started pulling pieces of tape off the walls and using them to hold the wires together as I twisted them around each other. *Twist the red wire to the other red wire. Twist the green to the other green.* The tiny pieces of tape held, but barely. I took the phone off the receiver again and put it to my ear. I heard a dial tone, but if I moved the headset much I would lose it. I quickly entered my inmate number and did what the operator told me. I dialed my girlfriend, Diamond Smith.

"Mercedes!?" she said in a cracked voice. "Why are you in jail? I got home to cops surrounding the house, and nobody was home except the kittens. There's blood everywhere. Are you hurt? What happened? I can't—"

I had to interrupt her. "Diamond, I'm okay. Calm down. I honestly don't know what's going on, or why I'm here."

I heard her start to cry. I looked around the room and realized it was as quiet as a nursery during nap time. Then people started whispering that the phone had been fixed. I turned back toward the phone box. "I need you to call my dad and let him know what's going on."

"What happened, Cedes?" she asked.

"Two guys kicked the door in and one shot Stacey. That's all I know so far," I answered. The static started growing in my ear. I looked down and found the tape slipping off the wires. "I don't have much time. The phone is broken. I tried to fix it but . . ."

The line was silent. "Hello? Hello?" *Fuck!* I put the receiver back on the hook and returned to my boat. Four women walked quickly to the phone and started arguing over it. I shook my head, knowing it wouldn't work. Five minutes after I put my head down, I got a tap on the shoulder. I looked up, wrinkling my brow.

"How'd you fix the phone?" a young-looking

white girl with long, blonde hair asked. "I really need to make a call."

"I just connected the colored wires," I told her as I put my head back down. A headache started creeping over me from all the loud talking echoing around the tiny concrete room. The light reflected off the bare walls, making the room too bright. I did like the rest of the women with no blankets. I tucked my arms into my shirt, curled up into a ball on my mat, and closed my eyes. *How did I get here?*

Chapter 2. Held In the Holding Cell

I was never one to pick a good group of peers, if you let my dad tell it to you. I was never a social butterfly, but I was friendly and approachable. I'd been friends with Stacey since the sixth grade, when we met in the cafeteria on the first day of school. I remember it like it happened yesterday. I walked in nervous and alone, and when I'd grabbed my food and gotten to the front of the line, I turned to the tables, and they were mostly full. I took small steps, not knowing where to sit down. It turned out my shoes had gotten untied, and I stepped on the string. *Bam!* My tray slammed to the ground, along with the rest of me.

A little mixed girl with short brown hair jumped up and ran over as I heard the laughter start. I felt my cheeks getting hot. I look up to find a hand reaching down. I grabbed it and pulled myself up.

"Are you okay?" She turned to the tables and screamed, "It's not funny!"

"Yeah, I'm fine. But the janitor doesn't seem fine." The janitor gave me a face as he approached my food, scattered all over the cafeteria floor.

Stacey laughed. She took me by the arm and dragged me to her table. "You can have some of mine. I had a big breakfast at home," she said as she guided me to sit down.

"Thanks, but no thanks. I kind of lost my appetite," I shrugged.

I never would have thought that day would bring me to the present one. We were best friends all the way up to tenth grade. After that, Stacey moved across town and had to switch high schools. We used to be together every day, and people started thinking we were sisters because we were both light-skinned, short, and always side by side. I never found anyone who could replace her, so we ended up finding each other again when we went to the same college.

By that time, Stacey was more into driving around town and meeting up with friends, while I was more into sports and studying. I was also tomboyish, while she was a pretty girl who always had guys laying out red carpets for her. After freshman year, we found a rental home that was within our budgets and not too far from campus. As soon as we moved in, Stacey found a boyfriend, who I rarely saw because he never stayed over or hung out at our place. Through most of sophomore year, I played basketball, and I had a lot of games, so Stacey and I barely saw each other at home anyway, except at the end of the day. Our classes were on opposite ends of the campus, too, so we rarely bumped into one another there. I remember missing her so much that sometimes I'd wake up in the middle of the night and just go lie in her bed with her as she slept.

The summer after sophomore year, Stacey told me she'd started taking Adderall to help with her classes. But I soon noticed that she was barely going to class. Everyday I'd wake up, go through my usual morning routine, and realize she was sleeping in. Sometimes she wouldn't get up until afternoon. After of few weeks of that, I started coming home to marijuana smoke so heavy it hit me like an electric bill in the summer as soon as I walked through the front door. I didn't complain too much—our rooms were far apart, so I would rarely see her. I still tried to hang with her, regardless of what she was doing, but I wanted to motivate her to get back on track. After I tried to convince her to go back to class, she started leaving home for days at a time. By that time, she was getting under my skin, never telling me when and where she would be. I didn't care the first few times, but when she started not being around to pay the rent, it got to be a problem. She would pop up five days after I'd paid it all on my own. That and not knowing her whereabouts was making my blood boil.

"I paid the rent already," I said, trying not to let my anger get to me.

"Well here, take my half, and a little extra. Love you, kid," she said as she kissed my cheek. She gave me an extra three hundred dollars.

Confused, I looked up at her. "How? And where?"

She just smiled and walked into her room.

A few months later, when we were still on the same page, she came into my room one Saturday and showed me her new driver's license. It was a California license; we were in Louisiana.

"Why California?"

"Because me and my boyfriend are going to move there soon," she said, smiling at her license.

I didn't really have anything to say to that. I was already hurt by how distant we'd become, and now she was telling me she was moving across the country. I definitely didn't like her boyfriend at that point.

From that day on, we kept our distance and barely said two words to each other. Though it's not like she was home enough to say more anyway. For a time, she started spending a week in California and then a week in Louisiana. I would have to feed her two kittens, even though she knew I hated cats. She kept them in the spare room, which had their food, water, and litter boxes, but she never fed them enough to last a week, so they would start meowing and crying loudly till I had no choice but to check on them. Once, she left for a whole month, and I felt so sorry for the kittens that I just let them roam around the house, which they were usually only allowed to do when Stacey was home.

The day of the home invasion, Stacey had been back from California about five days prior. I still didn't know if she'd gotten in contact with her boyfriend, or even if he was still her boyfriend. I also have no idea where or how Stacey was doing after the invasion.

I got up from my boat and casually walked over to the phone to try to fix it again. I got a dial tone and called Diamond.

"Hello?"

"I don't know what's going on, but I know I need to get my stuff out of that house before Stacey tries to take everything and sell it for her refugee trip back to California," I told her in a panic.

"Your dad thought of that already and I heard Stacey left the hospital. Rumors claim she made it back to California," she said. "But your parents and I started taking things out after you were arrested."

"Okay, thank y'all so much. Please let them know how much I appreciate them. And you. I knew Stacey would run off, though," I said in a cracked voice. I cleared my throat so nobody would hear my sadness. As I looked around, I saw that all the eyes were on me for being able to fix the phone and use it.

The line started making cracking and static sounds. "The phone might disconnect," I said. "I love you, I'll call you as soon as I can," I told Diamond just in time before the phone broke again. I felt my heart break a little at not being able to hear her tell me she loved me back. I left the phone and got back in my boat. Once again, some women tried the phone after me, and it failed to work for them.

I woke to the loud noise of the door popping open.

"Breakfast! Chow! Wake up!" The officer swung the door open and stepped to one side to let the trustee enter and hand each of us a tray of food. *My first jail meal*, I thought to myself.

The trustees wore gray suits instead of orange like the rest of us. They had jobs and stayed in a separate pod.

I took my tray and sat in my boat on the floor. The tray itself had to be about two inches thick, and heavy, given the little scoop of food. Today, breakfast was two little pancakes, syrup poured directly onto the tray next to them, and a sausage patty. The pancakes were tough and floury, and the syrup tasted like watered-down honey. The sausage was the only decent part, but it quickly gave me heartburn. I only finished half of my food. I looked around and found that half the women had pushed their food away and the others had demolished theirs within minutes.

"Y'all newbies better get ready, because this is probably the best breakfast day on the menu," a skinny, middle-aged woman announced.

The trustee started calling for the trays to be passed to the door. As one woman walked up, tray and cup in hand, she tried to step over a boat and tripped, sending food and juice spattering everywhere. Several women cursed as it hit their boats and blankets. The woman nervously grabbed her own blanket to clean the juice up before it could spread. The red juice left large stains on the floor even after she wiped up the liquid.

If it stains the floors like that, I can only imagine what it's doing to my stomach. I sat up with my hands wrapped around my legs. *It's fucking cold*! Trying not to shiver so much, I lay back down and rocked myself in an attempt to warm my body.

I look up at the only actual bunks in the cell and saw two heads under one blanket. I hadn't seen their faces since I'd arrived. But it was hard to see faces at all unless it was chow time, because everyone mainly slept.

I assumed the day would be just like the night, but I was wrong. Daytime was way louder, and you could hear movement outside too, as if there was an interstate on the other side of the door. Men were fussing and fighting next door, new inmates were crying hysterically as they entered the building, and officers were bickering with each other and the inmates. I saw a few women stuffing toilet tissue into their ears to block out the noise.

As I started to fall asleep, my arms wrapped around myself in an effort to keep from freezing to death, the door popped open. The officer brought in another orange boat and directed the inmate to put it in the little area right in front of the toilet. There was no other space for it. *Gross. How are people supposed to use the bathroom without stepping all over her?* Embarrassed, the girl set her boat down, lay down in it, and covered her face with the half-blanket they handed her. I was jealous of her blanket.

I tried to fall back asleep in the cold cell, but I was shivering so much that my armpits were starting to drip sweat and my chest began to sting a little. *What the hell is going on? Is this hypothermia or something?* The cold just wasn't treating me right at all.

I heard keys in the door again. My heart had started racing every time it opened loudly, like miniature heart attacks. The officer walked in with a basket full of sheets and blankets.

"Everyone without a blanket, come and grab one."

I got up and took a blanket and a sheet. They looked like they'd been taken right off of someone else's mat, with holes and stains all over them. I didn't care, with how cold I was. I wrapped myself up in both the blanket and the sheet and lay down to sleep until the next chow.

Every time the toilet flushed, it half woke me up. I felt bad for the girl in front of it. She kept her head tucked into her blanket, which seemed like the only way to avoid all the smells of other people's waste. It was already hard to avoid the smells in such a confined area. You could catch at least a whiff of everyone's pee, and especially of everyone's turds.

The keys jingled in the door again while I was halfway asleep.

"Pack y'all's things!" a female officer said as she propped the door open.

Everyone hopped up and started picking up their stuff. The officer showed us where to put the orange boats and mats, saying we'd be getting new mats at the women's pod, and told us to bring everything else—our blankets, sheets, plastic cups and sporks, and the miniature toothbrushes and toothpaste tubes we'd been given after processing. We held our belongings close as the officer started shackling us one by one.

"Could you give me a hand?" she asked a nearby officer who wasn't doing anything.

The other officer came over to help. "Lift your left leg. And now your right leg."

Damn, these shackles are cutting my ankles.

Once we were all shackled and cuffed, they put us in a single line and the officer started hooking a length of chain to our ankles that linked us together like a train cars. I looked up at the clock, which read 8:00 a.m. She pulled the first person toward the door I'd come in by. Outside, a white van was waiting. She motioned for us to take seats.

"Ouch! Pick your fucking feet up!" a woman yelled back to the prisoner behind her. It felt like knives slicing you around the ankles when someone didn't pick their foot up at the same time as everyone else, and the whole line would feel it.

"Which route are you taking?" the officer holding the door asked the one who was escorting us.

"It's a big load, so I'm taking them straight to the women's visitation door."

Once we were all inside, the officer pulled out and went right around a curve to a building in the back— the women's pod. She walked us out of the van and through a glass door. I read "Visitation" all around the room. Our officer waved to others inside a tower that had security cameras and controls. Then we heard a "beep" and loud metallic sounds from the door as it unlocked.

We walked into a room with another locked door four feet away, and the officer motioned for all of us to scoot inside so there was room to close the first door and unlock the second. Once we were through both of them, we faced a circle around a tower, which had a locked door but windows all around it. Inside, you could see all the security cameras for all three units. As I watched, an officer zoomed in on one camera so close that I could read the title of the book the inmate was holding.

As our handcuffs and shackles were being removed, another officer came out of a door that read "Classroom." She handed us each a mat and two rolls of toilet tissue.

"I'd hide my tissue as soon as you go into your dorms. That's the first thing they steal from you," she warned us. "Mercedes Flint, you're housed in unit 101, bunk number 22."

I looked toward the door that read 101 and saw a mixture of faces.

She made me line up by the door with the other women who being housed in 101. An officer put her hand on the handle. "One-oh-one!" she yelled, as an officer in the tower pressed a button to unlock the door. As she opened the heavy door and moved aside, we were welcomed in by forty faces that all read, "What the fuck do you want?"

Chapter 3. Poppin' in Gen. Pop.

As soon as we walked in, we all stopped to look at the bunk numbers, trying to spot our own. It wasn't hard, since all the empty bunks were shiny slabs of metal without big, green mats on top. Bunk 22 was closer to the right side of the dorm, opposite the toilets and showers. It was in the second row from the right wall and the second from the front of the day room.

The day room was what they called the front of the dorm. It had seven tables, with four chairs circling each one. There was a small television on the wall, and a microwave right underneath it. As I scanned the pod, I saw three phones on the right wall, across from the toilets.

The bathroom area was covered by two half-walls that you could see over. Inside, there were three toilets also separated by mini walls, and three showers next to each other, separated by walls and curtains. Near the toilets, there was a water fountain in a corner, where I saw two ladies refilling their water bottles. I finally spotted my bunk and started toward it. I noticed the other women following me.

"Damn, you fine as fuck!" someone at the tables yelled from across the room. I continued to my bunk.

I laid my flimsy mat down and started making my bed. I found I had a little drawer I could pull out from under the mattress, but all I had was blankets, a cup, a spork, and toilet paper. Remembering what the officer had said, I put my tissue in the drawer.

I heard keys in the lock. "Commissary, ladies!" an officer yelled through the hole in the door.

I knew I didn't have any commissary, because the officers in the intake building never mentioned anything about it, or said how to put money on the books to buy anything. Most of the women in the pod walked toward the door and stood around until their names were called. I sat on my mat and watched the person at the door take her commissary one item at a time through the window. She had a big, netted bag that she was stuffing her belongings into. I wondered how to get one of those.

"Do you know how commissary works?"

I looked up to a light-skinned, black chick with long, curly hair, big brown eyes, and a smile that showed she still had all of her teeth. She looked like she didn't belong here, but I realized I probably looked the same.

"No," I said dryly.

She grabbed my hand and pulled me toward a little computer screen by the pod door. She tapped it and the screen turned from black to blue.

"This is the kiosk. Type in your inmate identification number, and it'll tell you to make a password. Make sure nobody knows it," she instructed, turning her back to the screen. I typed a password in, and a list of item categories popped up. There was food, hygiene products, clothing, and miscellaneous items like games and dominos. I noticed a lot of things I needed as I scrolled through.

"Thanks for the help," I turned to say to the girl.

"No problem. I'm Jaylon Diggs," she said.

"My name's Mercedes, but you can call me Cedes," I said with a slight smile. I couldn't fight it—she had some kind of trick that made her smile more contagious than the flu in winter.

"Holler at me if you need anything." She turned and made a nice scene walking away, with the way her hips moved.

I got up right behind her and headed to the phones, but before I could sit down I heard "Bunk 22!" from the window.

I turned in confusion and walked toward the door.

"How do you have commissary and you just got here like ten minutes ago?" the woman who seemed to be in charge of the window asked as I walked up. The officer asked if I was bunk 22, and when I nodded she motioned the trustee to continue with commissary. I realized that all eyes were on me because I was the only new inmate that had been called for commissary.

Jaylon walked up behind me as the trustee started passing things through and handed me one of those netted bags. "You can use my bag to bring your stuff to your bunk," she told me.

I took the bag and started stuffing everything the trustee handed me into it. When we were done, the officer made me sign a paper confirming I'd received my commissary. The bag was full to the top. I dragged it to my bunk and opened the drawer to put everything in it.

"Damn, the lady that was in your bunk left yesterday. I guess they still took her money in commissary. You got real lucky," Jaylon said as she took her bag back. My drawer was full of flavored noodles, sodas, chips, candy, cookies, and bags of chili. I looked around and saw other women getting their noodles ready in bowls and standing in line for the microwave. It reminded me that I was planning to call my girlfriend and dad to put money on my books. I needed hygiene products and clothes, and now I needed a bowl to cook my food in. I went to the phone and dialed Diamond's number.

She answered before the second ring. "Hello?"

"Hey, babe. Just letting you know they finally brought us to population. Now I'm living with forty women instead of nine." She gave a fake, nervous laugh. "I hope you know I don't care for anyone in here," I reassured her.

"I know," she said with a sigh.

"I need some money for commissary. They wash whites and colors once a week, and I only have one pair of oranges and one pair of boxers."

She told me she'd put money in and call my dad for me as well.

There were a lot of passed-on conversations. The cost of one minute was twenty-five cents, which added up fast if you wanted to hold a full ten-minute conversation with someone. We hung up, and I went back to my bunk so she could call my dad and figure out how to put money on my books.

"So how long y'all been together?" Jaylon came around my bunk with a smile.

"Long enough."

"Think she's going to hold you down while you're in here?" she asked me.

I started to overthink, but I quickly snapped out of it. "Of course she is," I said confidently.

"How long are you here?"

"I'm not sure. What about you?"

"I'm here for a probation violation," she answered. "I'm waiting for my probation officer to get me released. I'm so ready to leave this shit place. It shouldn't be much longer."

We ended up talking for a couple of hours. Time definitely moved faster when you were talking or watching television. Not like there was much else to do.

"Rack up, ladies!" A new officer walked in and told us to get ready for shift change. We all got in our bunks as she walked through, calling our names to make sure everyone was present. As soon as she was done, she walked out of the pod and then came back with a stack of papers and books. She started reading the names on the mail and handing it out. I noticed people getting books, too.

"We can receive books that your family sends from Amazon or bookstores," Jaylon explained when she saw the confusion on my face. *Definitely need to get some books sent.* I started thinking about how boring the pod was.

Lying in my bunk, I realized the woman above me had never gotten up. She was completely under her blanket, so I couldn't even see her face or skin.

I heard keys in the door again. *Must be dinner chow.*

"Red!" Jaylon yelled in my direction.

I felt my bunk move. Red must be my bunkmate. A pair of long legs draped over the side and hopped down without using the ladder. In front of me stood a tall, dark-skinned stud.

"What's up, roommate?" she put her hand out. As I shook it, she introduced herself. "I'm Tyra, but everyone calls me Red."

"I'm Cedes," I responded.

She intimated me a little by how tall she was, and she had a short haircut that made her look like an actual guy in the women's pod. Once she started talking, though, she revealed that she was a genuinely nice person in disguise. The way she carried herself around the dorm, I could tell she was in charge, or at least the other inmates acted like it.

Jaylon was at the front of the chow line, and she waved to me and Red to join her. Red walked over like this wasn't the first time she skipped the chow line. I saw disgust and annoyance on everyone's faces at our jumping ahead, but it didn't seem like anyone was bold enough to say anything about it. I didn't think much about it, since I was hungry and hated waiting in lines.

Today's chow was spaghetti, peas, a brownie,

and juice, served in the cup they gave you in the holding units. The juice never sat right with me since the incident in the holding cell. I never drank the juice since that day.

"Here." Red handed me a pack of the seasoning from the noodle packets. "It'll taste hell of better if you sprinkle some on it."

I took the seasoning pack and tried some. She was right. It was ten times better than in its original state. I still only ate half a portion. The seasoning made it better, but not as good as the food outside.

As we brought our trays back to the front, I saw Red talking to the trustee who was collecting them. The trustee looked around before giving Red a folded-up piece of paper.

As we made our way back to the bunks, Red walked up behind me, hopped up to her bunk, and started reading the slip of paper. Then she looked down at me and started pointing at people with her eyes. "That's the baby killer. That's the mistress killer, that's the meth head, that's old school. And then you have the homeless people that're always hanging in a crowd." Everyone looked so normal that you would never believe the charges.

"What are you here for?" I asked.

"Drugs and trafficking. What about you?"

I didn't feel like saying everything that was written on my disposition paper, so I just kept it simple. "Same."

"You don't talk much. I like that," Red told me. "So, anyone catch your eye?" she asked with a smirk.

"I have a girlfriend at home," I told her.

"So do I, but in here, I'm just jocing, really."

I asked her what *jocing* meant.

"It's like a multipurpose word. It's used to say you're doing time in jail, and I use it to mean that I have a jail girlfriend, just to make my time go by faster." She laughed and handed me the paper. "This from my li'l joce across the street," she said as she pointed toward the pod door with her eyes. I assumed she meant across the hall in one of the other pods. "I make the trustee bring our dike kites back and forth," she explained.

Dike kite was just slang for letters from girlfriends, but you could get put in isolation, "the hole," for moving anything between pods that wasn't approved by officers.

"You only got one joce in here?" I asked her.

She gave me a big smile. "Nah, I have one in each dorm. I keep my time busy when I'm not in here sleeping."

She called to a girl three bunks down the row from us, a short, white girl with long, blonde hair. She walked over to our bunk with attitude. "What the hell do you want?"

"Why you acting like this in front of my new roommate?" Red asked with a grin. "This is Cedes. Cedes, this is Payton. She's my li'l baby," Red said, wrapping her arms around the other girl's neck.

Payton moved out from under her. "I saw the trustee give you that kite." She rolled her eyes and walked off.

"She'll be back talking to me tomorrow. Watch," Red said, laughing. She nodded toward Jaylon's bunk. "I see Jaylon has a little interest in you, though."

I look up to see Jaylon smiling at me and turned away shyly. She was pretty, but I wasn't going to be there long enough to even talk to someone, let alone catch feelings for someone. Or that's what I thought. Boy, was I wrong.

With nothing but time and energy, Jaylon and I started talking a lot more. She was funny, sweet, and mean at the same time. She started sneaking over to my bunk at night and clowning around with Red and me until we all fell asleep. Normally, Red would fall asleep first, and then Jaylon and I would do some friendly flirting until the 3 a.m. count. After a few nights of that, I was starting to look at Jaylon as my own li'l joce. I felt guilty about Diamond, but I couldn't talk to her about jail. She would get an attitude and tell me she didn't understand anything I was talking about, then we'd sit on the phone in silence and just waste minute money. In the end, I'd always tell her that I'd just call her back. But Jaylon understood everything.

"Cho-owww, ladies! Chow!" As the officer dropped the heavy, steel chow window open, I jumped out of my sleep, mad about being woken, mad about the December cold with no heaters, mad all over again about how I ended up in this situation. I threw off my blanket that felt like thirteen Taco Bell napkins full of holes and bent over to look under my bunk for my orange slippers before putting my bare feet or my fresh-out-of-commissary white socks on the cold and dirty concrete.

Walking toward the chow line with

disappointment written all over my face, I joined the early birds in the line, listening as they conversed in ripe morning breath that made me catch an attitude with everyone.

"Cedes!" I heard, in that voice that always made me smile.

As Jaylon waved at me to skip the line, I walked past angry old ladies with no teeth before catching up and standing in line behind her. Knowing my breath was hotter than hell in July, I hugged her from behind and avoided speaking directly in her face.

Not only did you have to force yourself up to eat at 4 a.m., but you were only given ten minutes to get your food, no matter where you were in line, and to eat before the call came for trays to be picked up. There was no way you could squeeze in time to get to your toothbrush and toothpaste.

It didn't take us long to get our trays after cutting into the line. We sat down at our normal table, the one furthest from the toilets, which went off constantly during the wake up hours. I wiped my state spork off with a piece of tissue I'd brought from my bunk, and then threw a sporkful of eggs into my mouth. I tasted powder, like chalk in egg form. It was weird and disturbing. I switched up and went for the grits next. The grits tasted like plain old grits, which met my expectations, since all I saw were commissary-bought sugar shakers in half of the hands in the chow line.

"Y'all want some sugar?" a middle-aged woman leaned over and looked at our faces for an answer.

"What you want for it?" Jaylon asked.

"Nothing. Newbie just looked like she needed it after the face she made." The turned back to me.

"Yeah, I'll take a little." I grabbed the shaker out of her hands quickly, shook sugar onto my grits, and passed it right back. The grits were still disgusting. I stood up and grabbed Jaylon's tray and set it on top of my own, then walked back to the trustee who was calling for the trays.

Chapter 4. Behind the Curtains

Every day it seemed like something new was happening in the dorm. If it wasn't new people coming in or old people bonding out, it was drama.

"I can't fucking believe this shit!" I heard the woman Red called the "mistress killer" cry out while she was on the phone. Her group of friends ran over to hold her as she cried. "They just locked up my boyfriend! He's in the other side of the building," she said between sobs.

From what Red told me, the woman had a boyfriend on top of being married to a guy already. The boyfriend also had a girlfriend, and the mistress killer had done exactly what Red said. She killed her boyfriend's girlfriend.

At the same time, the pod door popped open and a new set of women came in. It was only three women, coming from intake. One of them walked in and went straight to the bathroom.

"Aye, that's my girl," Red said, smiling and walking fast to the toilet to meet her. They talked while the other woman was sitting on the toilet, and then Red turned to wave me over to meet her. Suspicious about why we had to meet at the toilets, I walked over. When I arrived, the girl looked like she was digging around in her vagina.

"I got it," she said, pulling a small baggie out of her vagina hole. I know my face had disgust all over it.

"I hate to introduce myself like this, but I'm Mariah." She was a white woman, with short, blonde hair.

"Cedes," I responded, still trying to grasp what I'd just witnessed.

"She's a regular here, in and out like a McDonald's drive-thru," Red explained.

Mariah laughed. "Except I go to McDonald's by choice." She quickly stuffed the bag into her bra and walked us out toward her bunk.

"Go tell the Baby Killer that Red needs a piece of wrap," Red told me as she pointed toward bunk six.

I headed over and repeated the message. The baby killer pulled out a black bible, turned to the blank pages at the end, and ripped one out and handed it to me. When I got back to Mariah's bunk, she was breaking down the marijuana she'd pulled out of the baggie. I'd only smoked maybe twice before, at home with Stacey, but jail was boring and it was suddenly a lot more tempting. Mariah rolled up and told Red she was ready. Red went to our bunk and pulled out two batteries and two razor blades. Then I followed them back to the toilets. As I was studying engineering, I could already see what they were going to try. We sat around the toilet closest to the wall at the end, low enough for our heads to be hidden behind the half-wall.

"You have any idea how we're going to light this?" Red looks toward me.

"It looks like you're going to stand the batteries on the stainless steel toilet to ground them, and put the razors blades on the ends. Then it should spark when you tap the blades together." I answered a little too fast.

"Damn, you're smart as hell. I'm still learning to get the spark right," she said in a surprised voice.

I took the batteries and razor out of her hands. I set one battery on the toilet with the negative end sticking up and the other battery with the positive end up. Then I held the blades on both batteries with my thumbs and touched them together. With a light popping noise, a spark appeared. Red leaned over to catch the next one on the joint and it lit right away. She took two puffs and leaned toward the toilet bowl to release the smoke. Mariah flushed the toilet, and the smoke was sucked in. They passed it to me and I followed suit. I took two puffs and passed it to Red, then blew the smoke in the hole. Red put the joint out and stuffed the remaining half into her sock. We got off the floor one at a time to look less suspicious.

Damn, I have the munchies. Noodles just wouldn't fix the situation. I started thinking about all the snacks in my drawer. As soon as we got to our bunks, Red and I both dove into our commissaries and pulled out chips and cookies. After we snacked, we fell asleep until dinner chow.

The next morning, I woke to a burning smell. I sat up in

bed and saw smoke coming from the microwave. As I watched, the "baby killer" rushed over and pulled out a hand-rolled joint. I wasn't sure what was in it, but it smelled weird. Apparently, if you manage to light joints with the batteries and razors, the other way was to use the microwave. That seemed like an easier way to get caught.

The baby killer kept running back to the toilets where her crew were waiting, then getting back up and going to the microwave again. After about five attempts, she walked over to my bunk.

"Cedes, if I gave you the batteries and razors, could you light this for us?"

"She ain't smoking that damn orange-peeling joint," Red said.

Orange peelings? "Y'all really trying to get high off of orange peelings?" I asked with concern.

"Man, that's what cigarette smokers do." Red laughed as she waved the girl off.

Jaylon walked toward us, looking back at the orange peeling joint and shaking her head.

"Y'all not going to hit them oranges?" she joked. We both looked at her like she was crazy.

I barely touched my dinner. I still wasn't used to eating between four and five o'clock. But as seven or eight o'clock approached, my stomach would start growling. I checked to see if I had money on my books. A hundred dollars. I thanked my girlfriend and my dad in my head. I had enough food, so I ordered some shirts, two bowls, a radio, batteries (for the radio), soap, deodorant, a regular-sized toothbrush, a name-brand toothpaste, and a laundry bag to hold my commissary, since my drawer was full to the top. Commissary only came once a week, on Wednesdays, so I wouldn't get my bowl until tomorrow. I got my clothes ready and took a shower.

After dinner chow, it seemed like everyone had showering on their minds. "I got shower two after Payton!" I heard other people starting to call for the line to the showers.

"Let's hit the showers," Red said as she grabbed her towel from her bunk and started toward them. I grabbed my towel and followed. Red skipped the line for chow, so I knew she'd be skipping the shower lines too. She started undressing, and I did the same.

A woman named Amy came out of a stall and yelled, "Out of shower three."

"Cedes is hopping into shower three, for whoever thought they were next," Red yelled back. I heard a few women suck the only teeth they had in their mouths. Noticing all the showers were taken, I asked Red which she was going into.

"I'm hopping in with my li'l joce, Payton." She turned toward the pod door to see if any officers were watching. When it was clear, she ducked and crawled into the middle stall.

I was kind of curious what Red could do in such a small space, but I was sure the mind could come up with a few things while you were locked up in jail. Before I'd finished undressing, Jaylon walked to the first shower, cutting past someone else. "I'm next."

She was already half-naked as she waved to the

woman to wait. It was hard to not stare, especially because she was practically stripping for me. She took her clothes off slowly, making eye contact with me while she took her panties off, and I lost track of what I was doing. I finally stepped into my shower, and I got out around the same time as Red and Payton. After drying off, I put the same clothes on that I'd been wearing for my whole stay. Red had said they washed oranges on Fridays, so I didn't have too long to wait.

At my bunk, I found a dike kite on my blanket. It was from Jaylon. "I don't know what it is about you, and I've never even liked a girl, dated, or kissed one. But there's something different about you, and I'm not sure if we're even feeling the same way, but I just had to let you know the reason for my actions. It's kind of hard to stop it. It's natural. If you don't feel the same way and I'm just tripping, then just don't respond and we'll act like this never existed."

I smiled as I read the letter. When I glanced up toward her bunk, I saw her smiling back. I hope that gave her a hint to my answer. I pulled a sheet of paper out my drawer as the officer turned the bunk lights off. The day room lights were never turned off, so it wasn't completely dark.

"I do feel the same way. We vibe different, and it's not something I can fight any longer. But if we're going to joce off each other, we need to have an understanding. I do have a girlfriend at home, and this will probably never go any further than these doors. But I do want to get to know you more and hang around you more. It's something about that smile that just sneaks into my dreams at night, and it makes me ready to see the real thing in the morning."

I folded the paper up and looked toward Jaylon again, waving it so she could see that I wrote back. She pointed in the direction of the toilets. She wanted her letter, but after lights-out, inmates were only allowed to get out of their bunks for water and to use the bathroom.

I walked to the toilet closest to the wall, where there was a little blind spot that the cameras missed. I sat down while I waited. After a minute, Jaylon sat down at the toilet next to me. I handed her my kite and she gave me this big, pretty smile that I couldn't help but return.

"This is so new to me." She looked away shyly.

"Oh, so now you're shy?" I laughed, teasing her. Jaylon was usually outspoken and talked with no filter. She couldn't care less what anyone thought of her words. She also had a smart mouth for anyone who tried her patience.

I leaned in for a hug. I felt how tense she was, and I thought it was actually cute how nervous and shy she'd gotten. "You don't have to be nervous with me. I won't do anything you don't want me to." I looked her in the eyes as I said it.

"That's not the problem. I just, honestly, don't know what I'm doing, or how this goes," she admitted.

"Don't worry about that. Just do whatever you want. Say whatever comes to mind, and don't hold nothing back. We good." I smiled at her.

She gives me those "fuck me" eyes as she leaned in to hug me again. Then she got up and did her walk back to her bunk. I went back to my bunk and fell asleep with a big smile on my face.

The next morning, I slept through breakfast chow, but then I was awakened by a smell. It was as strong as ammonia and smelled like burning hair or something.

"Man, y'all starting that shit in the early hours?" Red screamed. I felt her body turning over in the bunk above me.

"What is that smell?" I asked.

"Them bitches in the showers burning off their pussy hair with some shit they buy off of commissary," she said with the biggest attitude.

To escape the odor, I ducked under my blanket and sheet, but it barely helped. It was definitely not the wake-up call I wanted.

Red leaned down from her bunk so I could see her face. "You wanna go hit the stick while they have the house smelling like skunk?" she asked, smiling.

I smiled back, and she took it as a yes.

I grabbed her batteries and razors, and we met at the last toilet. Half a dozen women were in the shower areas, buck-naked with whitish-blue cream all over their crotches. I got a spark from the batteries and pulled through the joint to light it, puffing twice before passing it to Red.

Jaylon wasn't a smoker, so she never came to meet us. She was still asleep in her bunk—one of the five three-tier beds, and she happened to be all the way at the top. I couldn't be that high up. I'd never want to come down. With all the times I get up to pee at night, I know my bunkies would hate me.

We finished our joint and walked out of the toilet area casually. You couldn't really smell anything over the burning hair. The women were finally wiping the cream off themselves and climbing into the showers together with no curtains to get all of it off. Red and I went back to our bunks to eat snacks as usual.

After lunch chow was served and picked up, commissary came around. I helped Jaylon with her big bag, throwing it up to her bunk for her, and I helped her organize her bunk until I heard my own number called, and I walked up to the door.

The first thing I was handed was my laundry bag, which I needed to carry everything else. Then I got the rest of list items one by one. I brought everything back to my bunk to unpack. On commissary day, it was a good idea to call the microwave spot as soon as things were passed out. Everyone would want to hit it with all their fresh food. The most popular thing while commissary was being passed out was to put Cheetos in a bowl, hot or regular, and microwave them for about a minute. If you didn't pay attention, you could easily burn them and make the whole dorm smell weird.

Finally having my own bowl, I fixed a bowl of noodles and sat down at a table.

"Next time, let me make you some noodles my way," Jaylon said with a grin. She went to her bunk to collect some items that people owed her. I didn't know the reasons behind those exchanges. When she got back, I cornered her against the wall and she looked me in my eyes. I scanned her entire light-skinned complexion, and then my eyes fixed on her pretty, pink lips. She started to bite her lip as I moved closer, till our bodies were fully touching. She looked me up and down while giving me her most flirtatious grin. Since she'd never been with a girl before, I figured I'd need to ignite everything and make all the first moves. I leaned in closer and grabbed her face to pull it to mine.

She closed her eyes as I planted my lips slowly on hers and softly sucked on her bottom lip. I felt her hands run down my back and around my waist, and she dug her nails into my skin. Our lips separated, and we both opened our eyes to stare at each other as if we'd both been introduced to new feelings. We smiled as I walked away from her.

I lay down in my bunk, still smiling. Her lips were magical, but I started feeling guilty about Diamond.

I heard the door pop, and an officer came in with the mail. When she called my name, she handed me a letter from Diamond and a book my parents had sent me. They knew how much I loved puzzles, so they'd sent me puzzle books instead of reading books first. I went back to my bunk to read the letter. Diamond talked about random things that were happening in the outside world. I was jealous at her mentions of food. Even though she wasn't a chef of any skill, she told me about places she'd tried in the city. Any food was better than the state tray or the noodles.

When lights-out came around, we all got ready for bed and racked up. At this point, the officers would usually come in to do the nightly count. After the lights were out and most of the inmates were asleep, I looked over at Jaylon's bunk to see if she was still up. She always seemed to be awake when I was. She smiled down at me and waved for me to come up. Usually she would come sit by my bunk, but it did make more since to go to hers, since it was against the back wall in most of the blind spots.

I got up, grabbing a roll of tissue just in case I had to act like I was going to the bathroom. I climbed up to the third bunk and lay under her covers with her, and we laughed and talked quietly. Every noise made me jump, though. This would be the most embarrassing reason to be sent to the hole. Jaylon must have liked the sample I left her with earlier, though, because after thirty minutes or so of talking, she turned toward me and came in for a kiss. We started making out, her hands running through my hair. My own hand started wandering as she put me in the mood. I could feel the heat rising from under her blanket. I slowly guided my hand down her curvy body and headed for her pants. Never unlocking lips, I slid my hand into her panties and start rubbing her clit. *She's so wet*. She let my lips go and silently moaned, and I could tell she was trying hard to keep quiet. I started rubbing faster as I felt her pussy dripping. She grabbed my arm and started to squeeze.

"Oh, fuck," Jaylon moaned lightly. I felt her tense up. After a few more seconds, her legs started to shake and her breathing got shallow. As she climaxed, she jumped a little against my hand where I was still rubbing her clit. She grabbed it and pulled it out of her pants.

"Oh my god." She turned to me. "What did you just do to me?"

I smiled back, knowing what my abilities could do to someone.

"I have to go clean myself," she laughed.

"Yeah, go wipe all thirty seconds off of you," I teased her.

She smiled as she rolled her eyes and we both climbed down from her bunk. Jaylon went straight to the toilet, and I followed a little after to wash my hands. When we both got to our own bunks, I looked back at her and caught her smiling down and blowing me kisses. I lay down on my mat and closed my eyes to fall asleep. After that night, I guess we were officially together as a jailhouse couple.

Chapter 5: "Joced Out"

After that night, Jaylon started smiling a lot more, and I'd always catch her eyeing me and biting her lip. She knew she looked sexy when she did that. The next week felt like only two days. *Damn, Red was right. Time flies when you're anxious to get up and see someone.*

When chow came around, Red and I met Jaylon at the front of the line as usual. This time, Jaylon backed up close to me in the line, and I grabbed her from behind and just held her. We tried to be inconspicuous, but it was tough to not touch each other. After that, we started growing a bond that was irresistible to me. Our laughs and jokes would turn to flirtatious conversations. We didn't want to be noticed by officers or inmates, though. When an officer noticed a couple, they would report both parties for sexual activity, which could give us more time or send us to the hole. So we'd mainly meet at the back wall by her bunk when we wanted affection. Red would bring Payton around, and it would feel like a double date in a back alley.

Those few days with my crew were the best I had arriving. I actually felt comfortable for once. Not comfortable being in jail, but comfortable knowing I had someone to confide in, comfortable letting someone make my time go by faster, and definitely comfortable sneaking around with Jaylon. The suspense was even sort of arousing. One night I was in Jaylon's bunk, just lying back and talking with her, and we lost track of the time. I heard the door pop, and before it could swing open I grabbed the rail and did a ninja jump, swinging my whole body down, and then walked casually down the middle row that led to the toilets. I turned back and Jaylon threw a roll of tissue to me. I caught it and started throwing it into the air to myself to play it off.

"Cedes, you're always up in the middle of the night," the officer said. "Stay in the bathroom until I finish the count so you don't mess me up."

The next morning, we heard shackles from the visitation doors. Some women walked up to the windows to see who was coming in.

"Is that Vanessa again?" I heard someone yell. A few women agreed and started laughing.

The door opened, and two new inmates walk in. One was a short white woman with black hair and big boobs. The other was a younger black girl with long, brown hair. The short woman went straight to her bunk to put her things down and then walked toward a table of women she seemed to know. The younger one stood at the front with her mat still in hand. She looked scared and lost. As I watched, a random lady walk up to her and asked her what bunk number she was in, and then she walked the girl to her bunk.

"Vanessa! What's good, baby?" Red called to the table.

"Ain't nothing. Same shit, different story," she called back.

Jaylon and I sat on her bottom bunkie's bed and talked for hours, as we'd been doing lately. Ever since the close call the other night, we'd also been writing letters.

"I'm extra tired tonight. We've been up the past seven days passing letters until four a.m.," Jaylon yawned.

"Good night," I said, and kissed her forehead.

I walked to the table where Red had gone to meet Vanessa. The conversation stopped as soon as I walked up.

"God damn." Vanessa scanned me from top to bottom several times.

"What?" I asked.

"I've never seen someone look as fine as you. No female has ever made me look twice."

"This my bunkie, Cedes," Red told her.

"I'm Vanessa," she said, as she reached out to hug me. She was a lot shorter than me, like she was fifteen, but with curves like a thirty-five-year-old. I didn't reach in, but I nodded.

"Oh, you don't like to be touched," Vanessa laughed.

"Just not by strangers," I responded with a smile.

Red and Vanessa got back to their conversation as I sat down with them.

"Yeah, me and Payton still in here jocing. She

mad at me right now, but the usual," Red said playfully, eyeing Payton from across the dorm.

"Anybody got smoke in here?" Vanessa asked.

"I was about to roll up right now," Red said. She walked to our bunk, and I went with her to grab the rest of the supplies for the smoke run. We all met at the toilet by the wall and we sat down next to it on the floor as I did my duties and lit the joint.

"Oh, so you're the hundred-percent lighter, huh?" Vanessa jokes.

"There's nobody better than Cedes." Red shoved me and laughed.

After getting two puffs in, we heard the locks on the door. Someone called *"Cooo, cooo"* toward us as a warning. I grabbed the batteries and razor and put them in my sock as I crawled to another toilet. Then I sat down like I was about to get up, flushed it, and walked out into the day room. Vanessa and Red both scattered around the day room as well.

The officer walked in. You could still smell the smoke, there was just no way to pinpoint where it was coming from. She made a round of the day room. It wasn't a count—she looked like she was on a mission to find something. Red made eye contact with me as we watched in confusion. After the officer finally walked out, I returned to my bunk to lay down to call it a night. Red hopped up onto her bunk and started rapping to herself.

Vanessa walked over to us. "What you think that was about?"

"I'm not even sure," Red responded and went back to her rap.

The next day, I didn't wake up until lunch chow, which was meat patties with mashed potatoes and peas. *I'm skipping this. I'll have some noodles or something.* It wasn't my favorite meal. As I watched the chow line get smaller and smaller, I grabbed my bowl and a pack of noodles from my drawer. I saw Vanessa doing the same. She beat me to the microwave, then glanced at my hands.

"No coke?" she asked me.

"Coke?" I looked puzzled.

"Give me your bowl." Vanessa snatched away my bowl and noodles. She started breaking down the noodles then and poured them into the bowl along with some Coca Cola. She popped it all into the microwave for five minutes and then brought the hot food back to my table.

"Try that out," she said with a smile.

I let it cool off before taking a bite of the weird combination. To my surprise, it was good. It reminded me of teriyaki–definitely an acquired taste, but at least it was better than the meat patties they were serving us. Vanessa smiles and walked away while she fixed her own coke-and-noodle bowl. I finished my noodles as Jaylon walked up and covered my eyes from behind.

"What did you just eat?" She looked in confusion at my empty bowl.

"I had some coke and noodles," I responded as I looked up at her.

She laughed in disgust.

"It's not as bad as you think," I said, laughing

with her. She sat next to me and we start talking like usual. The whole time, though, I felt someone staring at me. When I looked up, my eyes met Vanessa's. I turned back to Jaylon and tried to ignore Vanessa's staring.

"Who's that?" Jaylon caught on to my distraction.

"Some new girl." I brushed the question off, and we talked until Jaylon got up.

"I'm going to shower," she said, turning back toward me. "Are you coming?"

I went to my bunk to grab my clothes and started thinking about how the officer had come to check the dorm last night for no reason. I got a little paranoid, but I crawled into the shower right after Jaylon got in. Before I could even speak, I heard the door open. I looked up at Jaylon with wide eyes and quickly crawled out under her shower curtain and ducked into the next stall. A second later, my shower curtain was ripped down by an officer.

I turned around with my eyebrows raised. "You like what you see?" I asked, gesturing at my naked body.

The officer frowned, like she'd been expecting to catch me in the act of doing something illegal. She threw the curtain to the ground and walked away. Vanessa walked into the showers and picked the curtain up to hand back to me. She smiled as she scanned my naked body and then walked away.

Jaylon poked her head out of her shower to see what had happened. When she noticed my shower curtain, she asked "Did the officer do that?"

"Hell yeah. She thought she outsmarted me." I laughed as I put the curtain back up on my shower rod and we finished our showers separately. Jaylon and I got out of the showers at the same time, but she dried off faster than me and returned to her bunk, and not a second later, Vanessa walked into the bathroom area, making eye contact with me until she reached the sink. I shook my head and hurried to put my clothes on, then I walked toward my bunk where I saw Red sitting up on top of her own.

"You good?" I asked.

"Yeah, we just low on supplies. I need a new drop soon." She meant that someone outside was leaving some smoke somewhere for her. I never learned where her drops were or who was picking the stuff up. She hopped down and got on her knees next to my bunk. "Until then, I have us some Xanax and boost bars to hold us." She started chopping them both down on a book using her jail ID card, until she'd made about three lines of white powder. Then she called Jaylon to come over and snorted a line. I used to be prescribed Xanax, so it wasn't anything new to me, but snorting it definitely was. Before I could do a thing, Jaylon walked up and snorted her line like it was nothing. I followed suit and snorted the last line. I felt the powder clogging my nostrils, and I could taste the nasty Xanax flavor.

Red put her stash away and walked to the phone to call her girlfriend. Jaylon also left to talk on the phones. I lay down in my bunk and looked up at the pictures of Diamond I'd stuck to the bottom of Red's bunk where I'd see them right before I closed my eyes at night.

Just as I dozed off, I heard the door, and I looked

up with blurry eyes as about five officers entered with two K9s. I quickly sat up and tugged at Red's blanket, which was hanging halfway off her bunk. I felt her jump at the commotion and start looking through her bunk. Payton wasn't far from us, so Red threw a baggie of weed to her. Payton rolled her eyes and stuck it in her panties. I guess she knew the drill for this.

"Everyone to the showers for the squat and cough!"

All the officers started shouting. It felt like 2:30 in the morning. I saw Payton go to the toilet before she followed us in the line to the showers.

When I was next, the officer ordered me, "Take all your clothes off, turn around, squat and cough." She was the same one who'd barged in on my shower.

"I knew you didn't see enough of this body," I told her with a grin.

She rolled her eyes and told me to put my clothes back on and go stand in the day room.

After everyone was searched, they checked our bunks, having the dogs sniff every one. After they found nothing, they sent us back to our bunks.

"That's some hoe-ass shit," Red complained. "I had to flush the stash. I'll call in for another drop tomorrow."

Red and I lay in our beds for a while, just thinking. Then I sat up at the same moment she looked down at me. "Someone's snitching," we said in unison.

First the showers, and now the search. Someone was singing to the officers, and we were going to have to find out who. After that, Red and I got very paranoid, not knowing who to trust anymore. The whole next day, we just played spades and stayed out of the way. That night, we stayed sober, so we weren't too tired when the lights went out. I'd already kissed Jaylon goodnight, and she stayed in her bunk and went to sleep.

I stayed up with Red, Payton, and Vanessa. We were at Red's and my bunks, with the other girls sitting on the floor next to us. After a few flirtatious conversations, Vanessa brought up truth or dare. I knew right away that she was going to take advantage of the game to the fullest. Payton and Red agreed, so I guessed I was in too. Of course, they also added a rule that the first pick had to be a dare. When I got my first dare, Vanessa was already smiling. Payton was the one who had to give me the dare.

"I dare you to kiss Vanessa," she said.

I'd seen that coming since before we even hit the corner with it. I was never good with peer pressure, but once I set foot in jail, "you only live once" was the only rule I was going by. There wasn't much entertainment as it was, so I took part in most activities. My attitude leaned toward the wrongly-accused side of things, and how I shouldn't even be in this place. I glanced back at Jaylon's bunk and didn't see her sitting up or reading, so I figured she was asleep. By the time I looked back, Vanessa was already closer. I closed my eyes as she leaned in to kiss me. She grabbed my face and turned a simple peck into a full-blown make out. She wasn't better than Jaylon, but none of them compared to Diamond anyway. I missed her so much. It seemed like the game was just a set-up to get Vanessa and me to kiss, and then

Payton and Red, ending with a fuck session on Red's bunk. Vanessa's bunk was two rows behind me, right next to Payton's, so she would usually hang out with Payton. Vanessa was also a bottom bunker. Every time I looked at her, she seemed to be already staring at me and smiling.

The next morning, I slept in and woke up to Jaylon's pretty smile.

"Cedes, you never sleep this long. Are you hungry?"

"I am, but not for that food." I laughed and sat up. Looking through my drawer, I saw a coke and a noodle packet. I grabbed my bowl along with them.

"Where'd you learn that? It looks nasty as fuck," Jaylon said.

"I learned it from one of the new girls, who clearly isn't new here," I explained.

Today was visitation day, which also meant it was drop day. I saw Red trying to chat discretely with the trustees to see what positions they were working that night.

"I'm making the call for the drop," I heard her saying quietly. "It should be in the same place. The visitation trash can."

She turned to me. "You have some Xanax at home?"

I shook my head. I knew what she was getting at. She wanted me to have someone drop it off. The only person I knew who might understand coding would be Diamond.

I went over to the phones at the same time as Red.

"Hello, Cedes," Diamond said when she answered. "What's up?"

"I need a favor. I need a twenty-piece chicken nugget at visitation."

"What?" she asked in confusion.

"Call Red's girlfriend, and I'll call you back," I said, giving her the number.

Red eyed me as she listened. Then she turned to the trustee, who nodded to acknowledge that it was clear for her.

Jaylon came up behind me and gave me a hug. "My sister came to visit me," she said proudly.

I gave her a smile as she let go and walked to the pod door. As soon as the officer came to get her for the visitation, Vanessa walked up to me. "Your girl got a visit," she told me. I nodded and went to the table to write a letter to Diamond, since I hadn't written in four days. I usually wrote her a letter every day.

Vanessa sat next to me. "Are you waiting to get shipped to prison?" she asked.

"I hope not," I respond dryly.

"So when are you going to stop fucking with Jaylon and hop on a real team?" She gave me those big blue eyes.

I look at her and I laughed. "I don't even know you, and Jaylon would beat your ass, in case you don't know her." I started packing my writing tablet up. She watched me as I walked away.

I called Diamond to see if she'd gotten

everything straight, but no surprise, she still barely understood the mission. I just called it off in hopes that Red could get something through. I went back to my bunk and grabbed my clothes to take a shower while most of the inmates were out for visitation. As I started undressing in front of my usual shower, of course I saw Vanessa walking over too, the half-wall separating my naked body from hers.

"Would you like to take a picture?" I snarled.

"I'd prefer it live and in person." She leaned on the wall to admire me. I hurried to set up my shower curtain and get inside. But after about five minutes, Vanessa's naked body came under the curtain and into my shower. Before I could react, she grabbed me closer, staying on her knees. I looked down at her, trying to figure out what she was trying to do. I remember her saying she'd never been with a girl, but she sure seemed to know what she was doing. She put her lips on my clit and started to suck on it. My eyes rolled back. I'd never gotten head standing up, or even in the shower. I looked down at her again, and she looked back up at me as she went faster and faster, until I grabbed her head and held it as I started to cum in her mouth.

After climaxing, I pulled her head back, and she crawled out with her smile on her face. I was hoping some other inmates hadn't seen her enter my shower. If word got back to Jaylon before I could tell her, I just knew the pod would look like there'd been a shakedown. I felt paranoid, like everyone was staring at me, but that was normal.

As I dried off and dressed, I saw that visitation

was over. Jaylon waved at me from her tower. I put on my pants and bent over to grab my clothes off the chair in front of me. Before I left the shower area, Vanessa walked out of the first shower. She stepped out in front of me and winked. I brushed passed her as I heard the pod door pop open and Jaylon called my name. I also saw Red trying to get the attention of one of the trustees.

Jaylon met me at my bunk and gave me a big hug. "Are you okay?" I guess she could feel how tense my body was.

"I gotta tell you something before word gets around. When I took my shower, Vanessa came in and ate me out." I tried to just throw it out there, and I gave her a face of disappointment in myself.

Her smile turned into an angry mug with the eyes of a killer. She turned and started toward the showers, where Vanessa was still naked and drying off. I followed, trying to get in front of her, but she got to Vanessa first, who only had her panties and bra on. Jaylon grabbed Vanessa by the hair and pulled her into the shower.

"Cedes—that's mine. Don't fucking test me, because this would end really badly," she threatened.

Vanessa pushed her off and rolled her eyes. "She can make her own decisions." She grabbed the rest of her clothes and walked out, smiling at me as she passed.

The drama was overwhelming, so I went back to my bunk to lie down. I didn't look at Vanessa or Jaylon the entire night.

"You're not having visitors tonight," Red joked.

"No. I'm resting and gathering my thoughts tonight. What happened to the drop?"

"I'm not sure if the trustee has it or not. The law was on my tail. I'm going to find out tomorrow," she said. I felt her turn over in her bunk.

The next morning, the trustees did their usual duties, emptying the trash in the dorms, classroom, and visitation area. Red motioned to the trustee.

"She'll do a trash run this afternoon. Then you can talk to her," the trustee told Red.

I stayed in my bunk all day and wrote to Diamond.

At one point Jaylon came by and gave me those big, pretty eyes, which looked both hurt and happy. "I don't want you to think I'm mad at you or anything. You just have to let these hoes know who's for who around here," she said.

I wasn't used to the extra jail drama that came with this relationship. Given that you'd most likely never speak to any of these women outside the walls, they sure took the relationships in here as seriously as their outside relationships. I turned over to take a nap, my head hurting from all the drama and women's voices. Then I hear the door open and felt Red jump. She hopped off her bunk and headed toward the water fountain next to the closet door and interrogated the trustee. Jaylon and I slowly approached behind her.

"Where is it?" she asked, scanning the scared women up and down.

"It wasn't there. I-I looked exactly where you told me to look."

Glancing around the dorm with suspicion on her

face, Red slapped her hand down on one of the tables, waking everyone up who was still sleeping. I heard women silently smacking their lips and looking toward our huddle.

"The fuck y'all shoo-shoo'ing for?" Jaylon blurted at a group of staring eyes and moving mouths. That was the jail term for asking people what they were whispering about. I knew what was coming up next. There was only one other thing to do after your high was interrupted, and that was to replace the high.

I walked to my bunk to grab my grease bottle and took a freshly rolled stick that Payton brought back to us after the shakedown and stuffed it into my boxers. Well, I'm exaggerating about the stick—it was as skinny as a toothpick. As I collected a fresh pair of double-A batteries from my left-side bunk neighbor, I called out to Red that it was shower time.

As we met up, we heard all three showers running. Perfect for us, if not for the showering inmates. We went to each curtain to peek and see who was inside, checking for snitches who would sing louder than canaries at six in the morning. We picked one out, then I ran to the toilet with the batteries, razors, and stick to light it quickly and then crawled under the shower curtain.

"Scoot over, I'm under the water," Red told the inmate in the shower, Amy, as she tried to continue her shower with two guests in her square of space. We finally got two puffs each and put it out before the feens came around the half-wall like hound dogs at chow time. Red put the rest in her sock as soon as it was killed because she wasn't in the mood for sharing. High as kites, we dispersed to grab our clothes and went back to take actual showers. Then we lay in our bunks and floated to sleep as soon as our faces hit the imaginary clouds.

The next day, after lunch chow, Red and I sat at a table playing spades against some other women. We were using noodles to gamble with.

"I ain't scared, I got four noodles on the table. Let's go, who next?" Red shouted to the watching crowd.

"Me and Mary up next." Some old-schools sat down at the table.

"A'ight, Cedes. Let's beat these old bitches real quick," she laughed to me, even though we were both nervous, because the OG's were always the best with poker faces and keeping tricks up their sleeves. Red had taught me how to play spades. I used to watch my family play, but they were so advanced that they were throwing cards down and picking up them up faster than a speed boat, too quick for me to catch on.

"Clean 'em up this time, Cedes," Red said.

When we made a book, I would grab the cards and set them on my side of the table. Needless to say, we beat them and ended up with an extra amount of commissary.

"Cedes, you cooking tonight," Red laughed as she threw me all the noodles and other items.

I put them in my drawer. "What you feeling for? A potato log?"

"Hell yeah!" Red got excited. "Cedes is first in line for the microwave!" she yelled to the dorm.

I set up to start cooking. Potato logs were a process. I opened two bags of chips, added a little water to each, folded them, and set them flat on the table. Then I started smashing and flattening them till they each looked like one big rectangular chip. I mixed my noodles with chili and cheese, popped them into the microwave to cook, then spread the mixture on top of half the potato log and folded the other half across it. I added a little more chili on top, then sprinkled it with cut-up pickles and drizzles of ranch dressing. Jaylon taught me how to make potato logs the second week of being here.

After demolishing the meal, we both went to our bunks to sleep.

Chapter 6. Hole in the Wall

Click-click. That was the sound of the dorm door unlocking, along with the loud sound of bolts rubbing and followed by a *pop!* Then the door swung open. I heard everything in my sleep.

"Bunk 21 and 22, come with me."

Red and I rubbed our sleepy eyes with looks of confusion while walking toward the officer. From there, it was a long walk of shame through the halls in silence until we reached the warden's office. The officer called ahead through her talkie. "Are you ready for them?" Then the door swung open and I was face to face with walls of monitors and television screens.

The warden pointed to the two chairs in front of his desk, and we sat down, still gazing at every camera station. My hands suddenly started sweating and shaking a little, not knowing what was coming. Then the warden played a recording of my voice.

"Yeah, just bring me a ten-piece chicken nugget as soon as I get out of here."

"What's the address for the nuggets?"

I rolled my eyes as I heard myself say, "Call Red's girlfriend and get it from her."

The warden clicked a button and asked us, "Now who put the ten-pack of Xanax in the visitors' bathroom trash can?"

Red quickly responded, "How are we supposed to get to the visitors' bathroom from the other side of the locked doors?" She folded her arms across her chest.

I look at Red, my eyes saying *Damn, I've known you for three months and you're staying solid, while the roommate I knew for most my teenage years sang out my name to the government crew faster than Twista rapping to that song he made about women calling him Daddy.*

Meanwhile, the warden interrogated Red more because she was being the most hostile. As he yelled over her, *"You sent your girlfriend out to drop the package!"* Red folded her arms tighter and raised her chin higher, continuing to deny any part in the criminal activities, which never even seemed to exist to her. I was amazed to finally meet someone as strong-minded as myself—not snitching, but not admitting either. The safest way to go around the scenes without going back to the dorms as being a narc or a snitch.

The warden finally got tired of getting nowhere with us and ordered the officer to take us back to the women's unit. During the long walk back, Red and I looked at each other, smiling, while Red kept flirting with the officer to keep her from getting suspicious. When we reached the pod, the officer closed the door behind us and Jaylon ran up to hug us.

"What happened? Why'd the warden want to

see y'all," she asked with concern.

Red pushed lightly past her and walked toward her bunk. She needed her fix, but she knew it was too risky right now, when we were on the warden's radar. She sat up in her bunk and looked down at us. I turned back to Jaylon and told her what the warden had asked. Then I walked to the phones and called Diamond to tell her what had happened. But after I dialed, listened to every word the operator had to say, and finally got to the part where the phone calls the number, instead of ringing I heard, "Sorry, we cannot complete this call. This number is prohibited."

It felt like my head was filling up with fire. I dialed again and waiting for what felt like ten whole minutes until I got the same message. Panicking, I asked Red if she'd talked to her girlfriend yet. With wide eyes, Red jumped off her bunk, picked up the middle phone because it had the least static, and dialed her girlfriend. After a couple of minutes, she looked up at me and said "It's prohibited," then slams the phone onto its hook.

I knew it was about to be a mess. Red went to her bunk, grabbed her lotion bottle, and opened it up to an already-rolled stick. We never smoked in the daytime because it was too risky. During showers the steam would cover the smoke, but with this crew of officers, we weren't allowed showers before 4 p.m. Red called for me to grab the batteries and follow her. We walked to the very back of the dorm, where there were three screened windows that we could open slightly for a breeze and a whiff of the outside. We stood right in front of one and she pointed at the metal around the window. *Damn, she wants me to light the stick right here in the middle of the dorm*. I looked around at the cameras and realized we were in a blind spot. So I took out the batteries and razors from my pants and set them up to produce a spark. Red put the stick in her mouth and leaned toward it, then took two puffs and put her lips directly on the screen to blow the smoke out as she passed it to me. As I looked around while I took my first puff, I saw the feens looking up, their noses as wide as a tractor tire. I passed it back to Red so that when the feens figured out what was going on, they'd ask her for a hit and not me. She looked up and saw why I was so eager to hand it back, and she took one more big puff before she put it out as the feens reached our corner.

"Damn, y'all put it out already?" one of the older feens asked.

"This ain't Thanksgiving, man. It's not for the whole table," Red blurted at the old lady as she brushed passed her.

I too walked away and toward my bunk. It was barely noon and I hadn't talked to Diamond all morning. I knew she'd be worried. I never missed my calls to her: one in the morning, one around two or three, and a last one right before lights-out. My parents were just once a day, but that was usually in the morning. Thinking of my family, I hopped up, went to the phones, and dialed my dad's number, since he was usually able to answer his phone at work. Three minutes of the operator's voice and I got the same message. *Something's definitely up.* I tried the number again, and then I tried my mom. Same message. I even tried my two siblings, and none of my calls went through. *What the fuck?* I was getting aggravated and angry. I got off the phone and looked around. Most of the tables were full of women waiting for lunch. The rest were sleeping their lives away in their bunks. I spotted Jaylon at her usual table and walked toward her. She smiled when she saw me but quickly lost it when she realized my face was red with anger.

"What's wrong, baby?"

Before I could answer, the door clicked and two officers come in with cuffs.

"Bunk 21 and bunk 22, pack your bags!"

You only heard that for two reasons: you were going home, or you were taking the walk of shame. I knew for a fact that Red wasn't going home, so it seemed that we were about to hit the walk of shame that everyone talked about. We reached our bunks at the same time and both shook our heads, thinking the warden had pulled a stunt on us.

Jaylon grabbed me and hugged me tight with the saddest face. "Why are y'all going to the hole? How long are y'all supposed to be in there?"

Not having much to say, Red and I just said bye to Jaylon, grabbed the rest of our stuff, and headed to the door.

The walk of shame was more than your basic trips to the nurse or visitation, with just regular handcuffs. For this trip, you wore handcuffs that the officers hooked to a chain around your waist, which was also hooked to shackles on your ankles. To top that off, they also hooked you to each other like snow dogs. The route led to the nurse's station, except it went past, to a locked door behind a security camera station. It took about twenty minutes to walk the trip with shackles, handcuffs, and your mat, and carrying all your commissary in a big laundry bag. I can't imagine how much longer it would have been if we didn't have the laundry bags.

When we reached the locked door, the officer unlinked us but left the handcuffs and shackles on, and unlocked the door, which led to single units about as big as a baby's closet. *This is the hole*, I thought.

As soon as we started walking down the hallway, I heard screams, yelling and shouting, and loud cries. I wondered how it could be louder down here in the hole than in a room full of mad women. The officer opened doors 1 and 2 and directed us inside, then took our laundry bags and brought them to the other officer at the front of the hall to separate out what we couldn't have in the hole.

As we turned toward our doors, we said bye with our eyes. Then the officer shut us in the rooms. I turned around and saw a bunk, and right next to the door was the toilet, with a sink right above it. I heard mostly men's voices down the hall, so I assumed the hole wasn't segregated. Red was my left-side neighbor, and I could tell there was a man to my right. There was a little window right across from the door, but it was more screened off than in the dorms, and you couldn't open it.

I fixed my mat up with the sheets and blanket. I didn't have anything else, so I slept until dinner chow. Because the hole was next to the kitchen, we were fed at 3:30 p.m., and I was barely hungry, so I didn't eat. Shortly afterward, I heard the officer open the cell to my left. Red must've gotten her commissary back. Then I hear my own door click and unlock. The officer handed me my laundry bag, which was now half-full. The first thing I was happy to see was my $25 commissary radio, which matched the little radio I got after selling more than five items from a magazine issue for elementary school fundraisers. I put the headphones in my ears and turned the radio on to block out the talking and yelling from the hallway. All I heard was loud static. In the dorms, you only got good reception by the windows, so I walked toward mine and finally started hearing music behind the static. I pushed the radio against the screen and there was less static, but it seemed like that was the best reception I was going to get.

After a while, I noticed a faint banging through the music. I took my headphones out to see if I was hallucinating. But I wasn't—it was Red banging on the wall that separated us.

"Cedes! You good?" she called out. It sounded like she was close to the door, so I walked closer to mine.

"Cedes!" I could hear her loud and clear by the door.

"Yeah, I'm good. You good?" I yelled back.

"Yeah. This shit is shitty though. At least we have our radios to listen to, with sucky-ass reception." We both laughed, till we were interrupted by a noise like a train heading toward us in the hallway. I heard the chow window slide open next to Red's cell.

"Phone!" the officer called out to Red.

Five minutes later, I heard Red cursing at the

phone and slamming it back on the hook.

"Why'd you even bring me the damn phone?" she said as she slammed the chow window tightly in the door.

The train noise rolled closer to my door, and I heard jiggling at my chow window. It opened, and I bent over to look through the peep hole and see the officer with the phone.

"Phone!," the officer called, like I wasn't already by the tiny, rectangular window. I grabbed the phone and dialed Diamond's number. Same message. I tried all my family members again and got the same message. I saw what Red was complaining about, so I replaced the phone in its hook.

"Done already?" the officer said with a smile.

I slammed my window door shut. *Insensitive-ass officers*. I walked to my bunk and grabbed my radio, then I lay down across my mat and held it up to the window screen where I got the best reception, but my arm got tired of being held up. I wrapped my headphones around the radio to put them up and then sat up on my mat and looked around. I noticed a small hole in the wall to the cell on my right. It was too small to see through, but I could hear the movement from next door clearer than I could hear my radio. I wished it was Red in that cell.

I was getting bored a little too quickly, so I tried to go to sleep early. I'd say it was about six p.m. The sun was barely in the sky. As I drifted off, I heard a cry.

The sound got louder and louder. It was coming from the right-side wall. So I put my ear close to the hole, and to my surprise the cry became as dramatic as a hungry newborn having a nipple pulled out of her mouth. I was shocked to hear a grown man crying the way he was crying. I crawled back to my mat and lay on my back to fall asleep to my neighbor's crying.

The next morning, I was woken up at what felt a little earlier than the normal breakfast chow time. I heard Red's chow window fall open, and then I heard keys at mine. I grabbed my slippers and slowly walked to the door. I picked up my tray, and to my surprise the food was actually warmer than usual, which was a good thing because I had no access to a microwave like I did in the dorms. I ate the warm sausage patty and bland grits, and I wrapped the biscuit in tissue paper to save for a snack later. Then I lay down and fell back to sleep, planning to sleep the day away. I was tossing and turning when I heard keys jingling in my cell door. I sat up as it flew open.

"Come with me, inmate." The officer moved away from in front of the door to let me through.

"What's going on?" I asked him.

"You have a visitor," he said, dryly. I wondered if I would have to walk all the way back to the women's unit, but the officer brought me to a visitation hall right next door to the hole hallway. I hadn't seen or even known about this area. For some reason, it was much dimmer than the rest of the jail, which seemed like ten lightbulbs in a closet full of mirrors. The officer led me all the way down to the last visitation seat and window. I sat down and look through the window as I heard the officer walk out of the room. The door on the other side of my window opened, and my lawyer walked in and sat down in front of me.

"Hi, Cedes. How are you?" He smiled.

I looked at him with a confused face.

"So, your dad called me. He was worried about not hearing from you. And then they sent me to this side of the jail to see you in a different visitation room, which made me assume you are in the hole. Is that right?"

I shook my head.

"What happened?"

I didn't say anything.

"Do they have any evidence of whatever they're accusing you of?" he asked while opening the writing tablet he'd brought.

"Unless you call a ten-piece of chicken nugget enough evidence to charge someone, then no," I said sarcastically.

He laughed. "If that's all they have, then you won't be in the hole long. And also, I scored you a court date for next week instead of next month."

I thanked him, and the officer walked in to take me back to my cell. With very little to do, I did what I believe most of the quiet cells were doing—I went back to sleep. I did the same after lunch chow. Then keys unlocked my door and an officer opened it.

"Pack your things," he called out. I didn't have much to pack, since they'd taken most of my commissary, so I quickly gathered my little load.

I heard Red yell my name through her door as I walked out. "Cedes! You getting out?"

I yelled back that I was going back to population,

and that my lawyer had gotten me out of the hole.

The officer pushed me toward the front of the hallway, where they kept the "dangerous" commissary items. He pointed to a clear container of used razors, which were all the same color, shape, and size. "I'm good," I told him with disgust. After that he walked me back to the women's unit, but this time I wasn't chained to another body. I walked into the pod I was in before and was immediately greeted by Jaylon.

"Oh my god! I know it hasn't been long, but it was long enough for me to miss you! Where's Red?" She looked around me to the door.

"My lawyer visited me this morning, and I guess he made some moves," I explained.

"Well, damn. I'm happy you're back, though." She grabbed my stuff out of my hands and walked me to my bunk. I looked at the empty bunk above mine and felt guilty that Red was still stuck in the hole because she didn't have the money for a lawyer, but there wasn't much I could do from this side of the concrete walls.

I could barely sleep the night before my court date. Since the day I was taken out of the hole, rumors had been spreading from the other dorms that I'd ratted on Red, and that's why I was out of the hole and she was left back there. I couldn't even react to this, because it just didn't seem worth the drama, especially when I'd already told Red the situation

The time finally came around for me to get ready for court. The officers got me out of my dorm two hours in advance so they'd have time to shackle and handcuff me and put me in a chain with the other inmates. Once we were linked up like barrel monkeys, the officer escorted us to the white-out van. It literally had not a speck of color on it; just tinted windows. The officer opened the back and told us to get in.

Once we were inside, we hear the engine start up, and the ride-along started calling out names. As soon as the roll call was done, we took off for the courthouse. The insides of the windows were too tinted to see anything outside. The whole ride, we all just sat and stared at each other with anxiety as high as a crackhead without a fix.

After ten minutes or so, I heard the dispatcher telling the driver that court had been rescheduled due to some code I didn't know. I felt the van make a U-turn, and we pulled back into the jailhouse parking lot. Then we were put back in our pods with nothing but annoyance at the wasted time being shackled.

As soon as I walked through the door to 101, Jaylon welcomed me with wide arms. I missed her, but I missed Diamond more. Way more. Still irritated at not going to court, I headed to my bunk without saying a word. But before I could force myself to sleep, I heard the door pop open again, and an officer walked in.

"Bunk 15, pack your stuff."

I instantly opened my eyes and looked over. That was Jaylon's bunk.

"What the fuck? I have two months left. What do you mean pack my stuff?" She started fussing and walked toward the officer like she hadn't heard correctly.

"You're being moved to 102. Let's go." The

officer left to give her time to pack.

Jaylon walked over to me with watery eyes. "I don't know what the fuck is going on, but I will find out," she said in a cracked voice. Then she turned toward the full day room and yelled, "Let me find out if one of you bitches wrote me out of the dorm. I will make my way back and beat that ass too!"

I got up and walked with her to her bunk. I was regretting not speaking to her when I got back, because in a few minutes I wouldn't be able to hear her voice or give her physical affection anymore. I carried her commissary bag over my shoulder to the pod door. As it opened, she gave me a big hug and then yelled goodbye to some of her other friends.

I watched as the officer took her to the pod next door. All I could see of 102 was the straight line to the water fountain, and I could only see the door window of 103. I was relieved she was going to 102 instead of 103, but I was still upset she had to move. I started throwing chairs in the dorm and shouting that I was going to find out who was responsible. Nobody said anything or tried to stop me. Finally I looked up and saw Vanessa smiling back at me. I hoped she didn't have anything to do with this.

After throwing my tantrum, I tried to sleep to end this horrible day. I slept for maybe two hours, until I was woken up by an officer. I usually heard the door pop, but I missed it this time, and I looked up to an officer right in my face.

"You're rescheduled for court tomorrow morning," she told me, and handed me the new court disposition paper. I turn over and went back to sleep.

After about two days of not having Jaylon or Red around, I mainly stayed in my bunk and slept the time away. After I hadn't tried to call anyone in twenty-four hours or so, I decided to give the phone another try. To my surprise, it rang.

"Hello?" I could hear frantic panic in Diamond's voice.

"What's up? It's me. I miss you so much. It's crazy. All kind of things going on," I tried to summarize in a sentence.

"I miss you too. Are you okay?" Diamond asked with concern.

"Yeah. They put me and Red in the hole. My lawyer got me out two days ago, but Red's still in there."

We talked for our full ten minutes, and then Diamond told me "Call me back, I need to add money to the phones."

I felt guilty about all the money we'd spent talking, on top of commissary money. "'I'll call you back tomorrow, baby. This is starting to feel like a bill you have to pay. I love you."

"I love you too." I heard the sadness in her voice. We hung up, and I sat there for five minutes, lost in my thoughts. Then Vanessa walked up to me.

"You okay?" she asked.

I nodded and walked back to my bunk. For some reason, I kept getting a feeling that Vanessa was the reason for Jaylon being moved. As soon as I lay down, I heard the door open and saw Red walk in with her laundry bag. She hugged Payton before coming over. Then she hugged me and gave me a smile.

"Glad to get out of that shit." She hopped up on her bunk, and I felt her turn under her blanket. I did the same and fell asleep.

It's the morning of my new court date, they shackled, handcuffed, and linked us up just like before. I wasn't mentally prepared for the trip. For some reason, it felt a lot longer than the last time, even though we'd doubled our trip then. This time, there were only two women. We were put through the side door of the van, into a smaller area meant for only two people. The men were put in the back.

Some of the guys started trying to talk to the woman with me.

"Whatcha' in for, ma?" they'd scream out.

"Some stupid charge, what you look like? You wanna write me?" she yelled back.

Annoyed, I gave her a stare that said if she screamed in my ear one more time, I was coming out of these handcuffs and slapping her mouth shut. She must have caught on, because she stopped answering the guys.

Chapter 7. Taste of Freedom

We pulled up to the courthouse, and when the officers opened the door, my eyes instantly stuck to the suited-up officers standing around the van holding guns bigger than their arms. We each stepped down cautiously, trying not to cut off our ankles with the shackles on the long steps leading us off the van. The armed officers surrounded us as we entered the concrete building. We walked down a long hall to a glass door that they unlocked as they saw us approaching. We went through one by one, and they separated the males and females into holding cells. As they shut the doors, someone it the men's cell called out, "What time does court start?"

The cop at the desk replied, "You got somewhere

to be?" without taking her eyes off her computer screen.

I looked around and noticed how dirty the cell was. There was no toilet tissue by the toilet, no water coming out of the fountain, and not enough space to fit three people, but they put four of us in. The clock above the officer's said it was eight a.m.

I fiddled with my fingers for two hours and looked up when the door unlocked. An officer walked in with a box of brown bags and handed one to each of us. I opened mine to find a folded plastic bag holding two slices of bread and a piece of baloney, and another holding chips, a packet each of mayo and mustard, an orange, and a mini carton of apple juice.

After eating a baloney sandwich with chips inside, I sat up and let my eyes close. I dozed off for maybe an hour before I heard, "Come on, inmates." I jumped up and walked with my group to an elevator that took us up to the court halls.

"Everyone face the back wall until we reach our floor." There were actually signs on the back wall of the elevator that read *"Faces this way."* Once we got to our floor, we followed the officer down three long hallways until we reached a door that he opened into a courtroom with seats and half-walls between them. We each grabbed a seat and waited for court to start. I played with the handcuffs around my wrists to calm my nerves.

"All rise," the bailiff called out as the judge approached his stand and took his seat. Then he started calling out names and cases.

He finally called my name, and I stood and walked to the podium. My lawyer met me there and shook my hand in greeting.

"Mercedes Flint. Charges are possession of CDS1 with intent to distribute, possession of CDS2 with intent to distribute, possession of CDS3 with intent to distribute, possession of CDS4 with intent to distribute, three counts of possession of a firearm, and one count of money laundering." The judge looked at me with beady eyes. I couldn't believe all of those charges were being pinned on me without me having a clue of what happened in that house.

"We have been discussing a plea bargain with the district attorney. We are asking to reschedule, and then we will be able to make a plea," my lawyer said to the judge. The judge looked at the district attorney, who nodded in agreement.

"Very well then. We will talk again on October second," the judge announced, banging his gavel in dismissal.

I squinted my eyes at him as I walked off the podium. It was December. *This judge wants me to live with all forty of those crazy bitches for nine more months?* My body felt like it was on fire and being jammed into a three-by-two box. I felt pressure all around me, even though nothing was touching me but the cuffs and shackles. I could feel myself turning pale in the face and red all over my body. I looked toward the crowd of free people and saw the sad face of Diamond, who must have walked in right before my name was called. Her tears started falling as I walked toward the door I'd come in by, where the officer was waving for me to follow. It took everything in me to hold back tears of pain and anger.

I couldn't process what had just happened. The whole way back to the pods, I sat in silence, thinking about my next move or whether this was even really happening to me. As soon as I walked into my pod, I ran to the phones and called my dad. I couldn't even hold my tears as I told him that my next court date was in nine months.

"October?! Why does it take nine months to come back with a plea?" he said in a cracked voice, sounding like he was fighting tears himself.

"I don't think I can handle staying in here for nine months. Don't I have a bond? Can't I just bond out?" I asked him.

"I'm going to call your lawyer and see what's going on, and what we can do. Don't stress out. We're going to handle it. I love you. Stay safe, and call me in the morning," he said calmly, as he could hear me trying to stop sniffling after my cries came out.

"Love you too," I said as I hung up. I wiped my tears away as if I'd never been crying and walked to the day room to sit at a table by myself.

"Cedes, window!" someone by the water fountain called out.

Jaylon was in the window waving for me. She started window talking, but I wasn't too good at that. Window talking consists of mouthing a word while hand-signing the first letter. My eyesight wasn't great, so the whole thing was a challenge for me. I called Red over to translate.

"She's asking what happened in court."

I knew how to window talk, so I said I would write her, since it was a long story.

Red and I both walked back to our bunks and lay down to nap. But my mind was racing and I couldn't fall asleep. I got up and called Diamond. I knew she'd have more information about the outside world than I did, so I didn't hesitate to call. Normally whenever I was depressed or sad, I wouldn't call her. She could hear the pain in my voice, and I didn't want her worrying about me.

The next few mornings, I also called my dad a lot more than usual—at least three times. But "We're still working on it" was all I could get out of him.

Time was passing. It had already been a week since court. I was anxious about what my dad was getting done for me outside, but every morning I got less anxious, because my dad's voice was less and less excited with every call. I was losing hope, and I started preparing myself mentally for the time I would have to be in this place.

I calmed myself down by meditating on my bunk. I picked up the book my brother had sent me in the mail. It was an introduction to Buddhism and the afterlife. I must have read it about four times already, but it helped me with my meditation, and practicing Buddhism seemed to calm me down better than anyone in there could do.

A few more days passed. I'd stopped calling my dad about four days earlier. He hadn't done anything to upset me, but hearing the same old line and not seeing anything happen was messing with my head. "I'm working on it, real soon," is all he would say. I know it was selfish, but I had to hang up for my own sake. I was tired of the flavorless parish food, tired of being around so many women, and definitely tired of eating noodles.

"You look like you need another visit in the shower." Vanessa walked up to my bunk and sat down on the floor next to me.

"Is that your answer to everything?"

"No, but it might help for a moment," she said, looking at me with her big, pretty eyes. "Well, I'm here if you need me."

Red leaned down from her bunk. "You're not yourself anymore. Like your energy is drained."

"Because it is drained," I joked to lighten the mood.

"I'm going get ready for visitation with my brother. You going?"

"No. I won't let Diamond come up here after the hole situation. I'd rather play it safe," I answered.

"Damn, okay. I'll see you when I get back," she said. Then she walked toward the door as the officer popped it open and called for visitation. I turned back to Vanessa.

"You should come over to my bunk tonight. We can talk and get things off your mind," she suggested.

"I'll think about it."

I got up to play spades. We watched television at the same time. For some reason, the women just loved *61 Days In*. It was a reality show about men and women being paid to go undercover and stay in a jail or prison for 61 days to help authorities find the source of illegal actions behind bars. It seemed ironic that the women in the unit would treat new episodes like movie premiers— they'd call the microwave ten minutes beforehand so that everyone could fix their quick snacks, like cheese dip, chili, or popcorn. Then they'd move the first row of tables in front of the television and put the chairs in rows like in a theater.

I watched the show while playing spades, only halfway tuned in. I wasn't too proud to watch jail while being in jail. But it was funny when the people ended up tapping out after the first few days because they couldn't handle the small stuff, like jail food, jail showers, or just jail in general. In my eyes, though, the show was overrated and was making the women paranoid. They'd started claiming that some of the women in our unit were undercovers or snitches. Some women did show traits of being undercover, but not enough to really make those allegations. Besides, in the show the undercover agents were obvious because of how often they were taken out of their pods for interviews. Everyone knew that the only people who left the units daily were diabetics and people who needed regular medication. Apart from that, you weren't taken out of the units and walked to the back unless it was for court or lawyer purposes.

There was one inmate the women were certain was an undercover. She was new, and she always went on trips with the officers, but her excuse was that she was a military immigrant and had military court once a week. It was suspicious, but the rumors hit every pod, and she was labeled an undercover. Nobody would really associate with her after that.

I saw Vanessa go to the microwave and then turn around to look at me. After the microwave went off, she walked over. "Here, try these." She put a bowl of hot Cheetos in my face. They were actually hot from being cooked in the microwave. I didn't know why the Cheetos would taste different when heated up. I'd never heard of or seen anyone do that outside of jail, so I finally gave it a try. *Damn, this shit is good!*

I heard the door pop as Red danced her way back into the pod. She walked toward my table of spades and handed me a folded-up dike kite.

"From the missus across the street," she laughed, and walked back to her bunk to change out of her oranges. I left the spades table and followed her to read the kite, knowing how nosy other inmates would be if I read it in the day room. I started smiling as I read. I could hear Jaylon's voice saying the things she wrote.

"Better let them hoes know who you for." I laughed as I read, watching her handwriting get messier the madder she got as she wrote. She definitely made my day better, though. I wrote her back and then tried to figure out how and when she would get it. I looked up at Red, who was on her bunk reading a dike kite of her own she'd gotten in visitation.

"How you gonna give your letter out?" I asked.

"Chow. I already talked to the trustee who's serving tonight. You need a ride?"

"Yeah. Yours going to 102?"

"No, 103, but she'll gave it to Jaylon for you," she

assured me.

When chow came around, Red and I headed to the front of the line as usual. As the trustee handed Red her tray through the chow window, I started to talk to the officer to keep her from paying close attention.

"You're not eating with us?" I joked nervously.

As I was talking, Red put the letters under the tray before taking it out of the trustee's hands. Then she started rapping loudly as she walked off, and I walked up to the window next to grab my tray. We sat at our normal table to eat. When the trustee came back around to pick up the trays, she signaled to Red that the mission was completed. She also dropped a kite and kicked it toward our table.

Red picked it up and handed it to me. "M. F."

I walked to my bunk to put the letter under my mat and took my shower before the line got long. After showering, I lay down on my bunk to read it.

"I have court in the morning! My probation officer should be getting me out from my ninety day tech. Pray for me! I'll still write you and everything once I get out! I wrote my number at the bottom so you can call me! I'll be looking forward to that call, too. Don't let me down. Much love, Jaylon."

It was a bittersweet letter. I wanted her out of this place, but I also wanted her here with me to make my time move. I had to shake the selfishness off, and I walked to the window to see if I could get anyone's attention from 102. Ironically, Jaylon herself walked over to the water fountain where I could see her. When she was done filling her water bottle, she spotted me. She waved and blew kisses, and I did the same. I threw hand signs telling her I was happy for her and that I hoped she'd get released. She started signing back, saying I'd better call her and how she'd miss me. We said goodnight, waved bye, and I went to lie down in my bunk to fall asleep.

The next morning, I saw Jaylon walking out of her pod escorted by an officer to be shackled up for court. She waved at me with her handcuffs on and blew me kisses with the biggest smile on her face. I blew her a kiss back and threw prayer hands up with a big smile. Then I watched her walk out the front doors to where the transportation vans were parked.

Once she was out of sight, I started writing Diamond a letter, realizing I hadn't done so in four days. I normally wrote her every day but only sent them out every three days to save money on mailing supplies from commissary. After writing a two-page letter, I lay down and napped until I felt someone tapping me. I open my eyes to see Red.

"Ya girl back, doesn't look good." She pointed to the visitation door, and I watched the officer unshackling a line of inmates, Jaylon being the second one. I could tell she was crying while they were taking her handcuffs off. I went to the window and gave her puppy eyes as the officer popped open the door to her pod and let her inside. She looked at me and signed that she would write.

There was an AA meeting that night, and I knew she would be going. As soon as they brought the sign-in sheet, I made sure I was the first on the list.

"Put my name down too," Red yelled from her bunk, and I added her name under mine before walking away.

About an hour later, the officer picked up the sign-in sheet and called for the people on it. Red and I put on our oranges and headed to the door. The officer escorted us in the classroom pod by pod, so we didn't all get mixed in the room. Each pod was seated separately. But at the end of the meeting we were all able to stand up next to each other to hold hands and pray.

"God going to strike us down for using him to do dike activities," I whispered to Red.

We circled up and began to pray, and as soon as the speaker bowed her head, I looked across to Jaylon and saw her passing a kite to the woman next to her. As it moved around the circle, some women didn't want to take part, and Jaylon gave them eyes that could kill. But eventually one lady let it drop to the floor, halfway between Jaylon and me. Before the speaker said "Amen," I saw Red's long legs reach out and slide the kite back under her slipper.

We let go of each other's hands and sat back down until the officer came to collect us by pod. Red handed me the kite as soon as we walked into our own pod. I hurried to my bunk to find out what had happened to Jaylon. I'd never seen her cry, so my heart was broken for her even before I knew the situation.

"The judge said he found me guilty of the violation, and I have to proceed with my original sentence. I have two years DOC time, so I have to go to prison for some months. As soon as they calculate my time, they're going to ship me to prison."

I felt bad for her as I read. I wished I could give her a hug, the same way she would hug me when I had emotional troubles. After I finished, I walked to the water fountain to see if I could see Jaylon through the window. She was already waiting for me with a sad face. I sent her a heart with my hands and told her I wished I could hold her. We sat at the window talking for a little while, until the nighttime shift change. With certain officers, all the inmates had to rack up during count, and tonight we had one of those officers. Jaylon and I said goodbye through the window as we parted ways.

During the officer's head count, another officer looked in, saw what was happening, and waited to talk to the counting officer. Afterward, they met in the day room and exchange a few words. Then the officer who'd done the head count walked over to me.

"Pack your stuff."

I looked at her with concern on my face. I started packing, and Red hopped down to see what was going on.

"You're not going to court this late, and you haven't done nothing wrong. You might be getting out," she suggested.

I started to think that was what was happening. Word got out quickly, and as I walked to the window with my commissary bag, I found Jaylon already there, waiting to see where I was going. The officer popped the door open and said I wouldn't want to bring my food. I turned around and told Red she could take my commissary bag to keep. I just took my books and letters out first, before handing her the goodies.

"Hell, yeah! Stay safe out there, bro," she told me as she took the bag of food.

I signaled to Jaylon that I was getting out, and she jumped for joy while blowing me kisses. I never thought of giving her my number or address, since I was going home to Diamond. But I waved back as the officer escorted me to a door. It was the same door that led to the hall of shame, but this walk wasn't shameful.

"You're ready to get out of here, huh?" she asked.

"Yes. I'm ready for real food," I joked back.

We talked the entire way as if I wasn't an inmate anymore. We crossed the street back to the intake building, and she walked me to the office where I'd left my belongings. Once I had the things I was arrested with, like my clothes and phone, I quickly hopped out the oranges and threw them into a basket I was directed to. My old clothes were a long sleeve shirt and sweatpants, but since it was the middle of March now I only put the sweatpants on and kept my commissary white shirt on.

The wait to see the officer who would be releasing me was already testing my patience. My excitement was getting the best of me, and I couldn't sit down in the waiting room. I paced the floor about a million times before the door opened. Then I walked side by side with the officer to the desk where I would sign my release papers. After I signed them, she escorted me out the door. I saw my dad standing there with the biggest smile on his face.

I ran up to him and gave him a hug. "But how?"

"I paid for a bondsman." He hugged me tight. I knew that cost him a lot, as my bond was at least a hundred thousand dollars. It saddened me that he had to break his account for me, but I was too happy to be outside of those walls.

When we got home, Diamond was already outside my parent's house waiting for me. Before I could open the car door, she ran up and hugged me with tears rolling down her face.

"You can't ever leave me like that again," she said as she cried on my shirt. She wrinkled her nose. "You smell like stale feet." Then she grabbed my arms and looked me up and down.

We both laughed as we walked inside. The next person I was greeted by was my little sister, along with my mom.

They both agreed with Diamond about my smell, so I went to the bathroom to shower.

"Nobody wants to see all that," I heard my mom yell. I'd left the door wide open. I was so used to being institutionalized, I'd forgotten about doors and privacy.

My dad and I had a meeting with my lawyer and the bondsman the next day. The lawyer let us know that I had a court appearance coming in two months and advised me to stay out of trouble while he worked on some things for my case.

"The judge isn't too happy about you being released. I've been trying to get him to lighten up, and I'll continue that," he said.

I wasn't going back to my old home, where I was

arrested, but Diamond told me I could stay at her house, with two other roommates. That was better than being with my parents again, so I agreed. My parents didn't approve, I figured because they wanted to keep an eye on me. After all, they were the ones who'd worked so hard to get me out. I didn't want to be a waste of their money, so I assured them that I'd be okay. They weren't convinced, but they knew they couldn't control my actions.

I went to my old room, where my parents and Diamond had stored all my belongings from my old house. It looked like a storage unit threw up all over my bed and floor, but I couldn't be mad. At least I still had my stuff, thanks to them. I felt like a homeless person, not knowing what to do being back inside of a house with actual doors and more than four walls. I sat on my floor for a few seconds to gather my thoughts.

"What do you want to eat? I know you're hungry." My dad popped his head in my door.

"I want a steak," I answered.

"Put some clothes on. We'll go out and get steak."

I threw on what I could find in my junky room—a shirt and a pair of jeans. At this point, I didn't care what I was wearing, as long as it wasn't orange.

It was about two weeks before my court date, and my anxiety was higher than the Eiffel Tower. I just had a bad feeling about it, even though my family kept trying to keep positivity in my head. For some reason, nothing they said was getting through to me. My judge seemed to be more anti-drugs than most I'd heard about, and he also seemed to be homophobic. It was a horrible combination for my case. He looked at me like I was a felon, a criminal, or just plain trash. My lawyer put me in a "right direction" program. He told me that completing it and getting a certificate would look good in front of the judge. I didn't feel like anything would help unless I could change judges, but that didn't seem possible.

Diamond's place was very different from the home and roommate I'd had before. She'd simply moved in with a lesbian couple she knew for the time being because she didn't want to go back to her parent's house after the home invasion, and she definitely didn't want to stay in the old house. She'd been there for months now while I was in the parish jail. The house was definitely out of our comfort zone. We were used to a big room with internet, cable, and all the extras. This house was in an insect-infested part of the city. If you clicked the light on in the kitchen at midnight, you'd glimpse about twenty families of roaches scattering across every appliance. We tried to spend most of our time at work or in our room. We planned on working overtime to save up for our own place again, minus roommates.

"We'll have a place soon," I assured her.

One night as we were lying in bed talking about how jail had been, and how it was on the outside without me, I started remembering all the things I'd done in jail. It was eating at my conscience, and I had to tell Diamond. She noticed how quiet I'd gotten.

"What's on your mind?"

"I had a jail girlfriend." I looked up slowly while

saying it, and I could see the hurt in her eyes. A few tears dropped from them.

"The past is the past. I still love you."

A tear fell from my eyes too as I grabbed her to hug her. I felt as though my heart was broken with her, like I'd cheated on myself. The fact that she held me down the whole time and still wanted to be with me after I didn't hold my end down in jail only made me want her more.

After that, I started taking her out on dates and doing little romantic things, like running her bathwater after work, or cooking dinner and setting the table up like a restaurant before the roaches were up and roaming. I treated her like a queen, as best I could. She deserved it. She didn't deserve the hurt I'd brought her. We'd been together for three years, and I couldn't have wished for her to be anyone else. She was my one. I could felt it in my soul.

The time came for my day in court. I got dressed up nicely and walked alongside my lawyer into the courthouse. He opened the door to the courtroom we were appointed, and I walked through with him. I saw inmates sitting in their designated area like I had before. This time I was on the other side of the walls, with the civilians and the inmates' families.

"All rise," the bailiff called out as the judge approached and took his seat. We all sat down along with him.

"Mercedes Flint," the district attorney called out. My lawyer waved for me to come to the podium with him.

Then the judge called out my case. "Possession of CDS1 with intent to distribute, possession of CDS2 with intent to distribute, possession of CDS3 with intent to distribute, and possession of CDS4 with intent to distribute, three counts of possession of a firearm, and one count of money laundering." He looked down at me and my lawyer.

My lawyer got to work, saying a bunch of things that went completely over my head. My mind was too occupied by how so many charges were sitting in my face without my knowledge in my own home. I saw my lawyer's mouth moving without cease, and I saw the judge nodding nonchalantly.

"Do you accept the plea offer, Cedes?" my lawyer said, turning toward me.

"We are offering you fifteen years DOC, all but one year suspended, one year of parole, and four years of probation if you plead guilty to one felony count of possession of CDS1 and CDS2 with intent to distribute," the district attorney said to us.

My lawyer leaned toward me and whispered, "This is the best deal I could get out of them." It sounded like I would have to go to prison, but I didn't understand how I could be bonded out if I was going to be put right back in. "If you don't plead guilty and we have to go to trial, they'll give you the maximum sentence on every charge. And your chances of being found innocent at trial are less than ten percent," my lawyer quickly tried to explain.

"What is your plea, Flint?" the judge pushed me

to answer.

"Guilty," I stammered.

My lawyer grabbed my arm as he took my disposition paper from the bailiff, and we headed for the door. He took me to a table with a stack of papers in his hand.

"I know a lot of things were said that you probably didn't understand too well, so I'm going to break it down for you." I felt myself getting hot, as I knew bad news was coming. "So basically, he wanted to give you fifteen years, but he suspended all but three, which he wants you to spend in prison. The good thing is that three in DOC time really means one to three. You're only going to do about a year in state prison. And I did convince the judge to give you credit for time served, which means the time you spent in the parish jail will be subtracted from what you have to do in prison. One day in the parish counts as three days in prison. DOC will calculate your time after you turn yourself in, and once it's calculated they'll ship you to a prison of their choice. You'll be out in no time."

I knew he was trying to calm me down, as he could see me standing there in shock. He set the thick stack of papers on the table beside a black ink pad.

"I need your fingerprints on all four of these papers as a signature of agreement," he told me.

I did as I was told. All I could think about was having to go back to that place. My whole body felt warm and weak at the thought of returning to the parish jail. All my memories of the place started coming back into my mind. I tried to erase all my feelings or thoughts about it.

As my lawyer and I walked out of the courthouse and onto the streets, I was met by my dad and Diamond. They could tell by my face that I had bad news. I was holding back tears, not even wanting to say what was said in that room.

My lawyer beat me to the punch. "She has to do one year of DOC time, which with credit for time served should only amount to six months."

"What?" Diamond and my dad said in unison.

"She has to go back to jail?" my dad yelled.

"To be honest, with all the charges that landed on Cedes, it should have been at a five-year sentence. This was the best plea bargain possible," my lawyer explained.

I was still in shock and stuck in my thoughts. I couldn't believe I had to prepare myself to go back to that place. I hadn't been out for a full three months yet. The judge gave me thirty days to turn myself in, and of course I would wait for the very last day to do so.

Chapter 8. Straight to Pop

The day came that I had to turn myself in. I was told to be in the doors of jail by nine a.m. on October the first. I woke up early and arrived at seven. I had Diamond bring me, and my parents met me at the doors of the intake building.

As I gave Diamond a hug, her tears started to drop. "Why are they making you leave me again?"

I tried my hardest to keep my tears from falling alongside hers. I let her go and reached for my mom, dad, and sister. My brother resided in another state, so he was saying goodbye to me on the phone. After giving everyone a hug, I walked up to the front desk and gave them my name.

We went through the same motions as the first time. They even took new mugshots of me. After I changed into oranges and received my blanket and sheet, they seated me in the concrete square in the middle of the intake building where I'd waited to be put in a holding cell the last time.

Then an officer came up and started shackling my ankles. I didn't remember wearing shackles to go into a holding cell. She stood me up and walked me out of the doors that led to the women's unit. *Kind of glad I don't have to go to the holding cell.* We completely passed up the white van I rode in the first time, and instead she walked me to a side door in the building across from us. I was stunned by this new route to the women's unit. We walked through a locked door into hallways that looked like they went everywhere. Every hall led to more locked doors. Finally the officer stopped at one and waved to the tower in the middle to unlock it for us. It brought us to another hallway with a tower in the middle and male units all around it. We went through the next door, and it was literally the same as the hallway before. *These must be all the men's pods.* We walked through four hallways like that.

"Say, li'l mama!" the guys called out as we passed their pods.

The officer and I paid them no mind, and we reached a door that led to sunlight. I kind of remembered this route. It was like coming out of the hole, except with one less hall to walk down. We followed a walkway that was surrounded by a double layer of fencing, and it brought us to a secluded building. *The women's unit.* This must have been the back way. Or the long way, as my legs would put it.

"Pop open women's back door," the officer said

over her dispatcher.

When the door opened, we walked past the unit's windows to the pods. Women started coming to the windows to see what was going on, because usually intake came through the other side of the building. I heard shouting and banging on the windows. I guessed that was their way of intimidating people. The officer motioned for me to grab a mat from a pile of them that were just sitting around inside the door like stacks of flat, green boards. After picking out the fluffiest one, I followed the officer to a door that read "103."

It was the opposite pod from 101. Through the windows, I saw more gray shirts than orange. *This must be the trustee dorm*. Apparently, the women's unit was over populated, so the oranges were mixed in with the grays.

"You're in bunk 17," the officer said as she closed the pod door behind me. Once again, all eyes were on me as I walked through the room with my mat.

"Cedes?" I heard a familiar voice behind me. I turned and saw Amy in a gray suit. "You're back in here too, huh?" she said as she gave me a hug.

"You left and came back?"

"Yeah, I checked out to go to rehab, but now I'm back," she answered. I didn't ask for details, since her voice didn't sound inviting about it. "There's only one bunk open, and it's next to mine. Come on," she told me. She took my mat and walked me toward my bunk.

Amy was my left-side neighbor, and we were in the middle of the room, with bunks to the front, back, and on both sides. I looked around to see if I recognized any other faces.

"Red was shipped last week," Amy informed me. "None of us has heard from her yet." Amy and I didn't really talk about the last joce, but we had enough mutual friends to know a little about each other. She helped me make my bunk, and we both lay down on our mats. We chatted until I fell asleep on her.

When I woke up, I checked my commissary balance on the kiosk. One hundred and fifty dollars, from my parents and Diamond. I ordered most of the same items I'd ordered the first time. Last time I was here, I'd put on a lot of unwanted weight. I assumed it was from all the noodles and the state food. This time I decided to eat mainly seafood. I saw oysters and tuna fish on the commissary. *$3.50 for a little bag of clams, oysters, or tuna fish.* I knew that getting a week's worth would add up quickly, so I tried to get less clothing, as clothes were the other most expensive items. It was the middle of July, and the temperature in the dorms was definitely different from the winter. It was so hot that most of the women didn't have clothes on, and if they had their oranges on you could see their sweat stains as if they'd just run a 4K. Some officers were assholes and made us wear our full orange sets in the day room, and some couldn't care less if we were as naked as a newborn.

For some reason, this pod was hell of boring. The older women outnumbered the younger ones, and more than half the inmates were trustees who worked most of the day. That made the pod extra quiet and empty. The only pro of that situation was having the television mainly to yourself. Some trustees had jobs like going out to the fields to pick okra, oranges, or weeds. Others were on chow duty or cleaned the tower right outside the units. To me, they were the lucky ones. The hallway around the tower was well air-conditioned, like iced air. Meanwhile, in the units, we were sweating even while taking showers, since you couldn't control the temperature or pressure of the water. There was just a single metal button under the showerhead that you pushed, and the water was timed for maybe two or three minutes. It always seemed to be as hot as the building. Even the water in the fountain was warm. When it got too hot to bear, some of us would stand by the unit door to catch a cool breeze from the narrow gap underneath it. When the stricter officers were clocked in, they wouldn't let us close enough to the door to cool off.

A few days passed while I followed my routine and played spades with a new crew. It was usually Amy, her girlfriend, a white lady named Sarah, and me. Amy and her girlfriend were always partners, so I was stuck with slow Sarah. She was just too ADHD to play spades. She would start a conversation, and it would stop the game because she couldn't multitask enough to play a card, and we'd have to wait on her turn. Then once we finally rushed her to play and stop talking, she'd play a card that would cost us the game. Sometimes the whole table would walk off on her, because we could never finish a game. Everyone who knows spades knows that it's a fast-paced game that only requires shit talking, nothing more. We'd barely finish a game, and Sarah would run the crowd away as usual. So I also tended to my other activity to make time pass faster, which was sleeping.

I was woken up at two in the morning to the sound of my neighbor arguing with Sarah, who was in the row of bunks in front of her.

"Girl, you're trash in spades. Accept it and shut the fuck up."

"You'll have to shut me up then," Sarah yelled back.

My neighbor was a white girl who talked as urban as any white girl I'd ever met. She stood up, walked over to Sarah's bunk, and dragged her off it.

"Let's go. I'll shut you up real quick. Step into the day room," she said as she walked backward into the day room, setting up to fight.

The inmates who'd been awakened by the drama started instigating more than a drunk aunty at a family reunion.

"Sarah, get your ass in that day room! All that talk about how you can whoop anybody's ass," someone yelled.

"Nobody scared of her," Sarah said as she made her way to the day room and threw her set up to fight.

They circled each other with fists up until my neighbor threw her first punch.

Bop!

Sarah immediately curled up in a ball, while my neighbor kept throwing punches to her face. When she grabbed Sarah's hair to lift her face up throwing more punches, the officers finally flicked the lights on and rushed in. By that time, Sarah was lying on the ground holding her face and gushing blood all over herself and the floor.

They were both handcuffed and taken out of the pod. One of the trustees got out of her bunk, fussing while she cleaned up the blood on the floor. When four a.m. chow was being called, Sarah was walked back in looking like she'd been hit in the face with a fifty-pound bag of rocks. Her eyes were half-shut, her nose was crooked, and her mouth was busted. After that night, she didn't talk about how she could fight any more, knowing the pod would laugh more than they already were. She was the butt of jokes for two weeks straight.

Chapter 9. DOC!

Technically, I was still an inmate in the parish jail. I was waiting on DOC to calculate my time, and once I received it I would be on the next bus to prison. It had already been a month, though, and I'd seen two shipments leave the parish already. Meanwhile, I still needed the first step. Every time an officer walked in with papers, I'd get excited, but always for nothing. I felt like a toddler being denied the chance to play in the park. I knew my dad was making calls for me from the outside, though. I was called to speak with the warden about it.

"Apparently, your documents have already been filled out, and some reason they weren't shipped to the DOC center. Thanks to your dad's calls, I've sent it out. Now we just wait for them to respond," the warden told me. It wasn't what I wanted to hear, but it was better than no news at all.

Another week passed, and one day I saw a crowd of women run up to the windows. *Must be new inmates.* It wasn't all that interesting when new inmates came in, because then you had to get used to another face and body. You had to learn their ways and adapt to them. Everyone is different—that's the first thing you learned about women in jail. Nobody acted or thought the same. Not all women were clean or had manners, either. Some would sit on the toilet and take a shit without any courtesy flushes, or never brush their teeth, and the way some of them would adapt without any personal hygiene disgusted the hell out of me.

This time, three new inmates walked in the pod door. One was a tall, black woman with bald spots in her hair. She looked like the officers had made her take her wig off before coming in. The second was a short white lady with a boy's haircut. I assumed she was a stud. The last was a mixed, light-skinned chick with braces. She had a pretty face, but as soon as she walked in she started popping her mouth.

"I know that nobody better fuck with me while I sit my time," Brace-Face yelled before even finding her bunk.

Since my bunk was in the middle of the floor, I had a view of every angle of the pod while lying down. I watched the little stud sit in a chair close to the wall and fold her arms as she scanned the room. I watched the tall lady walk to the toilets, and I noticed that she went in without toilet tissue. When I heard the toilet flush, I looked back just in time to see her walk up to the sink, pull her orange pants down, and stick her ass in the sink to wash it.

"What the fuck are you doing?" a trustee yelled at her.

"Man, that lady's washing shit off her ass in the sink," someone else yelled, and started laughing.

"That shit ain't funny! I gotta go clean that shit

up, cause it's unsanitary," the trustee argued.

In my mind, everything in this place, including the people, was unsanitary. There was no fixing that issue. I turned to see Brace Face talking to a group of women she must have known already. Her mat was on one of the bunks right in front of me. I hated having new neighbors. You never knew how they would act at night, especially the first few nights. She sounded like she's been here before, though, so I started to worry a little less about her. I was more concerned about the stud, who still hadn't said a word. I watched as someone walked up to her to ask if she needed anything—since, apparently, the officers had run out of toilet paper to give out.

The stud shook her head no, and then as the other woman walked away, the stud laid her leg out and tripped her. The lady turned back as though she hadn't just tripped, and the stud cracked a smile as the other woman started going off on her.

"That's childish as fuck! How you just trip people like it's a joke, if I would have fell and hurt my damn self."

When she walked back to her own group and started complaining about what the stud had done to her, the stud stood up, walked to the pod door, and started banging on it. "I need tampons!"

The group of women started laughing. "They won't gave you any tampons here, you have to get pads."

An officer walked in to see what the commotion was about. The stud repeated herself, and the officer left the pod and came back with a bag of thick maxi pads. She handed three of them to the stud and told everyone else to line up for their two-pad-a-week fix. Amy usually grabbed my pads and toilet tissue when they were given out. After the officer left empty-handed, the stud walked to her bunk, two rows to the right of mine. She was on the second level of a three-tier bunk. She lay down on it and stayed there for a few hours.

Once chow came around, everyone got up to stand in line. I didn't leave my bunk. I had my oysters and crackers all ready for dinner. As I watched the women scramble into the line, the little stud joined them. She had blood all over her oranges. I didn't understand why she hadn't put a pad in yet. Then someone told her that she was bleeding, and all she did was laugh. As she walked up to the chow line, I saw people talking and staring at her. Everyone in front of her started to make space to avoid touching her. She seemed very weird, but I just assumed it was drugs. Most new inmates were coming down off some type of drugs.

"Ew, that's fucking nasty," I heard an inmate yell. As I watched, the stud walked about, sitting on almost every chair in the day room and spreading her blood around. The trustees would flip the room upside-down over that. The stud started laughing out loud as she saw everyone getting mad. Some women took their usual chairs and pulled them away as the stud continued to wipe her butt on random chairs. The pod started getting loud as everyone fussed with the stud, and all she did was laugh in their faces. I started to get irritated at all the commotion. Finally, I got up and started throwing every bloody chair at the stud. Amy and two other women followed my lead.

The stud started to get mad, breathing hard like she was ready to fight. Once her buttons were pushed, she started hollering loud as hell, and the officer ran in to see what was going on. As soon as she popped the door open, all the women pointed at the stud, and all of their mouths started moving at the same time.

"This nasty bitch is putting her period blood on all the furniture," a trustee told the officer.

The officer looked at the stud and told her to come to her. The stud got up and followed the officer out. They closed the pod door behind them, but we could see them talking through the window. I went back to my bunk and waited to see what would happen. Most of the others did the same.

Brace Face walked up to my bunk. "I'm Alexis. I just came out of the hole. They told me a fine-ass light-skinned stud would be in here." She smiled at me and fingered her curls.

"Yeah, that's the one right outside the door with the blood all over her," I joked.

"That's not funny." She rolled her eyes and walked back to her bunk and started fixing it.

"What were you in the hole for?"

"I wanted to check out of 101. They're dirtier and messier than any other pod. So I picked a fight and went to the hole," Alexis told me confidently. I could tell she was going to be the drama queen of the pod.

I heard something next to me and looked up to see Amy stirring up her whip-it. Most of the whip-its made in the trustee pod were Kool-Aid, coffee, and water shaken until it looked like whipped-cream coffee. They'd put a spoonful on everyone's hand to lick all day, and next thing you know all the women were hyped off of whip-it. I wasn't a big fan of the whip-its or the energy they brought to the dorm. It was even more annoying hearing the sound of the spoon whipping in the cup for two hours. I never understood how anyone could just keep whipping that stuff for hours until the texture was just right.

"Your wrist goin' fall off one day," I told Amy.

She rolled her eyes and offered me a spoonful.

"You're out of your mind, I don't want that shit." I pushed the spoon out of my face and she laughed, knowing I hated whip-its. We both turned our heads toward the door as we heard it pop open.

The stud walked over to her bunk and grabbed her mat and blanket. She was covered in blood, so everyone in her way eased right out of her way. They all started laughing and parading as soon as the door slams behind her.

I walked over to the phones to make my regular evening call to Diamond.

"What's up baby?" I heard her laughing with what sounded like a group of guys in the background. "Hey! I'm at work, everything okay?" she asked.

"Yeah, I just wanted to hear your voice," I answered. I listened closely to the background, trying to piece together every wrong scenario I had going on in my mind.

"Call me back later, I'm kind of busy," she said, hanging up before I could even respond. Something didn't feel right, and I wasn't with it. Even though it was already like an oven in the pod, I felt myself heating up inside. I started sweating more than I already was. It felt like even my ankles were sweating.

The next week, we get another load of women from intake. From my bunk, I could see past most of the women's heads that were planted in the window. There were about five shackled women around the tower. After the officers opened 101 and 102, they popped 103 open and two bodies walked in. One was a short, dark-skinned stud and the other was a tall, red-headed white lady. The white woman barely had all her teeth, but the stud looked about my age. About twenty-two. There was an open bunk next to me, the middle of a three-tier bunk, and another bunk was open by the left-hand wall. It wasn't good to be by a wall, because there were spiders, bugs, and mold all over them. I saw the stud walking toward my bunk with her mat, so she must be my new neighbor.

"What's up?" I nodded to her.

"Nothing much." She shook her head as she put her mat on her bunk.

"Be prepared for all these hoes to come up and ask you random shit," I laughed to her.

"Why would—" Before she could finish, several few inmates came up to the bunk asking if she needed any toilet tissue or hygiene products.

"They wouldn't ask you if you were ugly," I shouted over them.

The stud laughed and walked around the crowd

of women to my bunk. She wasn't the prettiest, but in jail, any "boy" who walked in was considered fine or fuckable.

"They thirsty as hell in here," she told me.

"Yeah, it'll be like this the first few days. What are you in for?"

"Probation violation, a thirty-day tech. Waiting for court to see what happens," she answered.

"You shouldn't be here long then. What's your name?"

"Ro. And you?" She reaches for my hand.

I grabbed and shook it. "Cedes."

The women had dispersed from her bunk, and she lay down. We chatted for a few hours, then Alexis ran up and gave Ro a big hug.

"Cousin!"

"What the hell are you still doing in here, Lex?" Ro fussed at her.

"Long story," Alexis said. "I'll tell you later."

As she walked back to wherever she'd come from, Ro and I returned to our conversion. We found out that we'd played basketball in the same league and might even have played each other a couple of times. We were too young to remember exactly how we'd first met on the outside.

"Yeah, y'all's team was good as fuck," I told Ro.

"Man, you was the coldest on your team, though. I was just placed on a good team." She laughed.

I spent even more time at my bunk after Ro was checked in. All we would do was lie down and laughed about random things all day. Alexis would turn around in her bunk to face us sometimes and join in.

Once Ro mentioned that she'd violated her probation by submitting dirty urine. "I popped a Xanax the day of a random piss test," she said, rolling her eyes. "This is my second time violating. I was supposed to be off about a year ago." She told me how she'd never been in jail longer than a month and a half. "Damn, I don't remember it being this hot the last time I was here." She started fanning herself.

"Yeah, for some reason it's bad this year. Like, wanna kill yourself bad. The women are funky, the heat gives them attitudes, and the showers are hotter than these bitches' breath."

Ro laughed. I wasn't lying, though. I was just trying to make the situation sound a little better. It was literally too hot to fall asleep sometimes. The only time it felt cool was when the sun just started to rise, which confused the hell out of me. I kept expecting it to cool off around one in the morning, when the sun was nowhere to be found. I was always wrong—it always felt hotter when the sun was down.

Ro only had a month in here, and she treated it like a vacation. She had four girlfriends, two in our pod and one in each of the others. I had to window talk for her since she didn't know how.

One morning, I was awakened by a loud *bang!* I thought it was a gunshot, which took me back to my old house with Stacey. My eyes flew open, and I saw this middle-aged woman opening and slamming the drawer in her bunk. It sounded like someone kept firing a shotgun next to my head. I heard other women groaning and smacking their lips. I didn't know what was wrong with the lady, but she was a trustee who had to wake up for morning chow to get ready for work. She was clearly making all the noise on purpose, I just didn't know her purpose.

My heart still racing, I threw off my blanket and stood up, along with two other inmates who were fed up with the slamming. Ro was one of them.

"Man, what the fuck is your problem?" We all started fussing at her.

"Fuck all of y'all," the trustee said as she walked to the line of other trustees at the door, waiting to go to work.

Normally, when the trustees come back from working outside around two p.m., they all shower and lie down to take a nap. But since this trustee'd woken up on the wrong side of the bed, the non-working inmates had other plans for her. I heard several women plotting. "We not letting this bitch sleep, since she had the nerve to wake the dorm up just because she had to be up."

The trustees always ganged up with each other. If they didn't like a certain orange-shirt inmate, they could easily have her written out of the pod. So gray mainly stayed with gray and orange with orange.

I stayed in my bunk most of the day. When two p.m. came around and we saw the trustees coming back, everyone started going into the day room and getting loud. The trustees walked in and headed to their bunks to grab fresh clothes and take showers. I suddenly remembered how it had felt being scared out of my sleep, with the PTSD I still had from the night Stacey was shot. My anger took over and I walked into the day room too and started throwing chairs around.

"Since it's fuck us, fuck y'all!" I screamed.

Some of the other orange shirts followed me and started banging on things to make it loud and uncomfortable. The trustees were so afraid, they wouldn't even step out of the showers, thinking we were coming for them.

"Now you see how it feels to have your heart racing and not know what the fuck's going on, huh?" I screamed at the group of them.

Everyone behind me started talking shit along with me. Then the door popped open and an officer came in to see what was going on. After she asked each inmate around her, she got everyone to settle down and made the trustee who started the commotion in the morning apologize to the whole dorm.

Afterward, the same trustee walked up to me. "I'm really sorry. I didn't think of how I must have triggered your anxieties. I just got some bad news and freaked out, and I wanted to apologize to you personally. Are we good?"

I turned my back to her and walked away. I wasn't good at letting things go, or even accepting apologies. I was better off taking a walk around the day room and meditating with my cheap radio in my ear, getting reception wherever I could.

"You good, my boy?"

I turned to find Ro checking on me. "Yeah, just tired of these bitches, man."

Ro was a funny-ass person who could make me

laugh at the worst times. But that's why I appreciated her, even though she got all the drama from being the dorm hoe.

Night came and we did our normal lights-out duties, stacking the day room chairs against the walls, mopping the floors, emptying the trash, and wiping the tables and chairs down. Ro and I being the bored, childish inmates that we were, we started messing around with random things, like picking up the lid to a commissary bowl and throwing across the room like a frisbee. We were jumping up on tables and flying through the air to make crazy catches. It was our way to tire ourselves out so we could fall asleep in that heat box. The officers in the tower were laughing at the stupid things we came up with to pass the time. It was entertaining to some of the inmates too, but the trustees were hating us by this point. We always interrupted their cleaning.

By the time we got into our bunks, we had a whole crew of women around us ready for our nightly clowning session or truth-or-dare games. Thanks to Ro and me, our section was like the club or the entertainment center. Trustees would get furious at all the laughing and giggling going down by our bunks. It was only a matter of time until one of them snitched, or at least complained to an officer about all the late-night activity.

Ro became my go-to person even though most of the time that meant I was translating girlfriend drama through the window for her. Finally I'd tell her I was taking off for the day and she'd have to learn to talk through the glass herself. I'd help her get her letters to her girlfriends in the other pods too. Every time she was talking through the window with other girls, her girlfriends in our pod would come over and fuss with her. I sat back and watched. I knew it was just entertainment for Ro, and I let her have her fun. Alexis would come up and clown around with Ro and all her girlfriends.

After about thirty days, I realized that Ro must be checking out any day now. Just as I thought of losing her, I heard a pop at the door, and an officer came in.

"Bunk 20, pack your shit." Ro flew to her bunk.

I went over and dapped her up. "Aye, be good. Don't come back here," I told her.

"And you be safe once they finally ship you." She came in for a hug.

I watched as she took all her things to the door and waved at her girlfriends in the other dorms. The two in this pod were both out for work, since they were trustees.

"Tell my girls that I'll write them and come see them! Make sure they put me on their visitation lists," she told me.

"I got you. I'm going to miss you on some gay shit, but get the fuck out of here, man!"

I watched her walk out of the door, doing her little dance as the officer shut the door behind her. She knew how to make a scene.

Days passed. One night the officer walked in with her stack of mail, and as usual most the inmates surrounded her waiting for their names to be called. Amy usually grabbed my mail for me. She was nice to me, like an older sister. When my name was called, she went up but the officer said it was legal documents that had to be put into my own hands. I ran up, thinking it was what I'd been waiting for.

It was. I read "DOC" across the top and then ran to my bunk to open it. I read down to find my calculation, and I saw "One year in the women's prison."

My head started flipping. I wondered how I hadn't received a shorter sentence after they'd agreed to give me credit for time served. As I scanned the documents over, I noticed the date of credit for time served was the court date from July. So basically, no time served from before that date. *They fucked me.* I had to go to prison for a year. Not knowing what prison would be like, I got nervous. I knew it would have ten times as many women as the parish.

I went to the phone and called my dad first.

"I have a year in prison," I told him a shaky voice.

"*A year?!* But you served months in the parish! The lawyer said it should only add up to six months more," he said, confused.

"They messed up the date when they started the credit for time served. They didn't use my arrest date, they used the date I turned myself in. So that made it zero time served from that date." I tried to explain without getting upset again.

"I'll figure this out. Call me tomorrow." My dad hung up.

I called Diamond next, and as soon as I told her the sentence, she started crying. I had to hold it together for the sake of my reputation in here.

Now it was waiting to get shipped. My motivation was shattered. I was just ready to get away from these hot-ass pods and dirty-ass bitches. The next morning, I heard someone call my name.

"Cedes! Ro outside!"

I ran to the window where you could see the visitation parking lot. There were two sets of fences separating it from the building, but you could hear each other if you yelled.

"Cedes, I miss you! Keep your head up, baby!"

"I will! Man, they gave me a year in prison," I screamed back to her.

"What the fuck?! Them hating-ass bitches," she yelled. "I'll be waiting for you when you get back, I promise!"

"Aye, either go to visitation or get out of my parking lot, yelling with my inmates!" An officer walked over and made her leave.

I went back to my bunk to literally sleep my days away. Eventually, Amy tried to make me get up and play spades.

"I don't want to be a third wheel with your girlfriend," I fake-laughed to her.

"Fine. I'll come and ask again in about an hour."

I fell asleep for the rest of the day and ended up staying up all night. I did some of my puzzle books and wrote a few letters to Diamond. Then I managed to fall back to sleep and not wake up until lunch chow. After that, I went back to my bunk for most of the day.

Alexis came up to me with tears in her eyes.

"You okay?" I looked at her with concern.

"It's Ro. . . . She overdosed last night." She started crying.

I grabbed Alexis and hug her tight.

"I'm so sorry." I tried to be strong for her, since that was her family and I'd only lived with her for thirty days. I just wished I could tell Ro thank you for the memories she'd left with me, and the time she'd made pass by quicker. She hadn't even been out a full week.

I stayed in my bed for the rest of the week, barely eating or sleeping, just lying in my bunk. Amy would try to make me talk, but I was as stubborn as a cow blocking the road. I wanted to sleep until my shipment day.

Chapter 10. The Shipment

Shipments were only done on Wednesdays, so on Wednesday mornings I could never go back to sleep after 4 a.m. chow. My name hadn't been called the last three Wednesdays, and at this point I wanted to leave the parish jail faster than the dinner chow line formed. I kept hearing things were better at the prison—like more women, bigger pods, and my favorite, two-person cells. I was so tired of hearing forty different mouths speaking during chow that I was hearing voices in my sleep. From the day people found out they were DOC, they started keeping their commissary packed in their laundry bags, just waiting to get shipped. They never tell you where you're being shipped to, but it always happened early in the morning.

"Concord, Riverbend, Tallulah, St. Gabriel, and Huntsville are the women's prisons they ship you to," one lady at my table mentioned during chow.

"I heard St. Gab moved all the women inmates to Tallulah or Concord," the lady on the other side of her replied.

I'd never heard any of those names before I was arrested. I didn't like talking about it because it made me more anxious to get out of the parish. Most days I tried to sleep away, or else I read books all day to keep my mind off the heat and off the wait.

After another four Wednesdays, my patience was running thin. The week before, I'd seen three inmates from other pods being shipped out, and the week before that, only two, both from our pod. Everything and everyone was aggravating me.

By Tuesday, I'd lost all hope of getting shipped. I proceeded through my regular activities, playing spades, eating tuna fish, watching television, and sleeping. I started to lose my appetite from the jail food, and I took to eating only tuna fish and oysters on saltines. I was still talking to my girlfriend every day, but I realized we had less and less to talk about. She'd started sounding less excited to talk to me, even though she still answered on the first ring. I waited for nighttime to come, looking forward to mail and more books that I'd asked my parents to send.

"Mercedes Flint!" the mail officer yelled.

I grabbed my stack of letters and books. I'd asked for these books a week or two ago, but all mail and books had to be checked over by officers, so the wait time was long. I was still on a cliffhanger over Diamond and the day she'd been "busy." I went to bed early to read the new letters from her. Diamond normally wrote more than she talked on the phone, so I was always more excited to get her letters than to actually call and talk to her.

After I read her letters, I started writing one back. Since I was sure I wasn't being shipped, I finally unpacked some of my items. I took out some pictures Diamond had sent me, and as I looked at them I smiled and missed holding her. I took some toothpaste out, squeezed a little onto the back of the picture, and pressed it to the bottom of the upper bunk, where I could see it as soon as I opened my eyes. I put up six more and smiled with satisfaction. Then I lay back down and looked up at the pictures until I fell asleep.

I slept right through breakfast and onward, until I heard an officer walk in and start calling out numbers. "Bunk 22, 25, 19, 17, 10, 6, 30, and 3! Pack your things!"

I started to rub my eyes as I heard excited voices mixed with crying ones. I hadn't really heard the bunk numbers, so I wasn't sure if I was being shipped or not.

"Pack your shit! We're finally leaving!" Amy shook me to fully wake me up. "She called bunk 17!" She started packing next to me.

I jumped up and began packing my own things. I pulled down the freshly hung pictures. The toothpaste hadn't even dried completely, so I put the damp pictures in one of my crossword books to keep from spreading wet toothpaste everywhere. Then I started throwing everything that was in my drawer into my laundry bag. I was able to fit it all in, though it was stuffed to the very top.

Everyone else who was being shipped had their double-stuffed laundry bags ready to go. We could see the officer pulling DOC inmates from the other pods and walking them to the classroom. As everyone started saying their goodbyes, the door popped open and the officer called our bunks numbers again to go through. With our big bags over our shoulders, we walked in a line to the classroom to be shackled and handcuffed.

"Stand next to someone you are comfortable being joined with," the officer suggested.

We all took the smart route and picked people the same size as us to avoid getting cut by the shackles. I was one of the shorter women, so I paired up with someone who was a little shorter than I was. We were shackled together at the ankles and hands, which made it ten times as hard to carry our laundry bags through doors and hallways. Finally, the officer gathered us in front of a big, white, tinted-out van and started putting our bags in the trunk.

The van had three rows of seats in the back separated by a gated window from the two front seats. The officer helped us climb inside, as it was hard to do while attached to someone. Three people could sit comfortably in each of the first two rows. The last row was a bit longer, and we tried to squeeze four into the seat. It was pretty squashed, so as the van left the building, I managed to slide my hand out of the handcuffs and sit on the floor, which was like a little aisle, and I could stretch my legs out and lie or sit more comfortably. The passenger-side officer looked back at me and shrugged in dismissal.

The driver announced our destination. "Y'all are being shipped to the prison up north. It's a five- or six-hour drive."

We all made noises of disgust. We were already cramped, and it was about seven in the morning. We also knew we wouldn't have anything to eat until we reached the prison. My stomach had already started growling since I'd skipped breakfast chow. *This is going to be the longest field trip of my life.*

I couldn't sleep at all during the trip, as I wondered what the prison would look like and how things would be living there for a while. I didn't know what to expect.

About seven hours later, and after the officers made a lunch-break stop for themselves at a gas station four hours in, the van stopped at a locked gate, which started moving after an officer called over her dispatcher. I put my hands back into my cuffs and sat up to look out the windows.

I saw fences everywhere and buildings all over the property. Once we got through the first and second gates, we pulled up to a small building on the side of some bigger ones. The officers came around to the side to pull our door open. After we stepped down, they walked us inside to a room with chairs. We found seats and started looking around. A woman in a different blue police suit walked in and sat at a desk across from us. She had a fresh wig on, with long, fake eyelashes and dark skin, and her clothes were as tight as the ponytail that was pulling her hairline back. A yellow badge was attached to her shirt. I assumed she was higher ranked than the officers who drove us. She handed us some papers that read "Rules and Regulations of the Prison."

After reading some parts of them aloud to us,

she stood up and motioned us to follow her through the door she'd come in by. We walked down a hallway to a locked door. As she opened it, a burst of sunlight flashed across my eyes. We emerged into a fenced walkway, and she guided us to a door on the left. "Classroom" was written on the door.

We walked into a building with rows of chairs facing the doors. Between the doors was a screen projector and a podium with a microphone attached. She walked us to the back of the room, where there was a gated door, and had us sat in the last row of chairs as she called us into the back room one by one.

"Mercedes Flint."

When she calls my name, I walked through, and she escorted me to a hidden bathroom and handed me a cup.

"Pee in this. Do not close the door, do not flush. There's a sink in there to wash your hands," she directed me. I was more than certain that my pee would come back dirty, but I was already in prison. *What more can they do to me?*

After the officer collected our pee samples, she came out to the front room and set up two tables that were folded in the corner. "When your name is called, meet me at the table with all your belongings and start spreading them out on it." Another officer walked in, went to the other table, and started calling names too.

"Mercedes Flint." It was the yellow badge who'd called me. I dumped my laundry bag of parish commissary out on the table. She started pulling my parish clothes out of the stack.

"You can't wear the whites or the oranges outside of the pods. I won't make you throw them away, but I shouldn't see them being worn outside," she told me. I nodded my head in agreement.

After going through everyone's belongings, they asked for our sizes and brought out boxes of yellow pants and shirts and white shoes. The yellows were fresh out of the plastics, but the shoes had clearly been worn before. After we got our two pairs of yellows and our beaten-down white shoes, yellow badge dismissed us to another inmate that she called the orderly.

"Okay, so I'm bringing y'all to the barracks, which is where intake stays before being housed in the compound where the big pods are," the orderly explained. "I'm bringing y'all to an empty pod to shower with special soap and shampoo for your hair. This is to decontaminate you of whatever someone might have."

We walked into a room full of scattered bunks with rows of tables by the entrance. The orderly walked everyone to the back, where there were three toilets side by side, and beyond them a square area with showerheads on the walls—two on the back wall, two on the left, and two on the right.

"Six people can shower at once," she said. She stepped back to set the shampoo and soap on the half-wall blocking the toilets.

After everyone had showered and washed their hair, we gathered around the tables at the front and waited for instructions.

"Everyone put their towels in this basket so I can send them to the wash." She said it twice for those who didn't hear. Then she walked us outside to show us our assigned pods. Other inmates walked closer from the other side of the barracks to peek at the new arrivals. I remembered Red being shipped and started to wonder if she would be here.

In the barracks, there were five pods called Foxtrot, Alpha, Beta, Echo, and Star.

"Mercedes Flint, you're housed in Foxtrot," the orderly read off the list in her hand. She brought four of us to the door of Foxtrot and then moved on with the rest of the inmates. I followed the crowd in, and we met a guard sitting directly in front of the door at the day room table. As I passed the guard, I saw a familiar face. Megan looked up and ran to me with the biggest smile on her face.

"Cedes!" she screamed as she gave me a big hug. "I haven't seen you since we were teenagers!"

Megan and I had practically grown up together. Our grandmothers were best friends. We were separated by growing up and life in general, though. We'd gone to schools on opposite sides of the city, so we hadn't run into each other since we were about twelve. Megan was a short, black girl with a short , brown fro. She was light skinned, thick, and had a pretty smile.

"What the hell are you doing in prison?" I asked her.

"I should be asking the same," she laughed. "My bunk is by the back of the first row, near the door," she told me as she glanced at the commissary bag in my hand.

"Mercedes Flint! You are bunk number 10," the

guard called out. She handed me a green mat that looked exactly like the beat-up ones in the parish jail, and with it a pillow. I was excited to have an actual pillow, even though it felt like cotton-stuffed plastic. It was better than using my folded-up parish blanket that had more holes than a cheese grater.

Megan looked back at the bunks and pulled my arm to follow her. "You're in the same row as me but way on the other side of the dorm," she said. I noticed that I didn't have a top bunkie to deal with, so I was pretty happy with the location. I saw the number 42 on the bunk closest to the door, so I assumed I was living with about forty women again.

"I've been waiting for months to get moved to the compound, where you have your own cell and only one roommate," Megan said, rolling her eyes. "But I'm glad you're in here now. Maybe it'll make time go by faster. Your bunk is right next to my cousin's—hers is the top left one right there. You'll meet her at lunch chow. She's probably out roaming around and violating rules right now."

I started to tie my commissary bag to my bunk as I looked around to see where people were putting their belongings. There were only two small drawers with a door that flipped up at the bottom of the double bunk. It was only enough space to hide my roll of tissue. I ended up stuffing my extra rolls inside both of the drawers, since I didn't have a bunkie.

"Hey, you want this bag?" I heard a voice from two rows down.

"You're giving Cedes your duffle?" Megan turned

to her.

"Yeah, I have another one coming, so she can have this one if she wants it," the woman said with a big smile.

"What do you want in return?" I asked.

"Nothing," she said, still smiling.

Megan turned back to me. "Damn, you getting a fan base already!"

We both laughed as I walked over to grab the bag from the little lady. It was a big, blue duffle bag that I noticed only a few people had under their bunks.

"You have to write the staff to get one of those bags, then you have to wait in line until they approve you to have one," Megan informed me. I was happy that someone gave me one, because I still had a full bag of commissary from the day before shipment. I started to move it out of the see-through laundry bag and into to the big duffle bag, which I could zip up and lock.

"Commissary is on Tuesdays, and money needs a least a full day to enter your account. And we have a long walk to the commissary building, so don't lose your laundry bag." Megan continued to update me on the facilities. "We also have a salon, and there's normally a barber in there. It's inmates, but I heard the dark-skinned chick was really good at fades and shit."

I wasn't planning to let anyone cut my hair, because I didn't expect to be here long enough to need it, even though I really was starting to need it about now. I finish transferring my stuff, and we went to sit in the day room. The dorm had three rows of long tables with bench seats connected to them. Behind that, separated by a half-wall, there was an area with three toilets side by side, and to the left of those three sinks and with silver trays as mirrors above them. Beyond the sinks, there was a silver square with two showerheads on each wall. It was different, having the guards so close instead of in towers where they couldn't really hear every conversation. Some inmates were surrounding the guard, laughing and joking with her. A few more walked in, and the dorm seemed to get louder and louder.

"Danielle!" Megan waved at someone in my bunk area.

"What's up, cuz? Who's this," the girl said as she walked up to us.

"Cedes, this is my cousin Danielle. Danielle, this is my childhood friend, Cedes."

"You're pretty as shit," Danielle said to me. She stepped closer and looked at me from top to bottom a few times.

"She don't want your ass, sit that down," Megan laughed.

Danielle was the same height as Megan and me, and caramel-colored with dreads that she seemed to have just started growing.

"Y'all hungry?" Danielle asked as she started back to her bunk. "I was about to make potato logs before the line for the microwave gets too long. "Mrs. Ma'am, do you want a potato log today?" she yelled to the guard.

"Hell yeah, I want one. Danielle is first on the microwave!" the guard yelled to the pod.

"Of course we want one," Megan yelled too. "She makes the best potato logs out here," she said to me, turning back. I'd learned to make potato logs in the parish, but I was trying to stay away from all the noodles. It was hard not to eat something that was practically thrown in your face, though, so I ate the potato log that Danielle used her time and commissary to fix for us.

As the night grew shorter, I went to the phones and called Diamond. "Hey, what's up," I said, as she answered on the third ring.

"Nothing much, just working."

It was still awkward to talk on the phone, so I kept it brief to not waste money on silent calls. After hanging up, I called my dad and told him how different it was in prison. "I know this is only the beginning of it," I said to him.

"You're going to be fine. Just let me know when we need to put money on your books. I've also have been talking with your lawyer, and we're hoping to get some good news soon," he told me.

I knew he just wanted to keep sending me positive vibes, but things always seemed to move slowly while I was behind these walls, so I didn't cling to any new information he gave me. I'd just let it brush past to avoid unnecessary excitement.

"You wanna shower with us?" Megan whispered as I was listening to my dad. "Me and Danielle normally shower at eight, before the lines get long. Even though we still go when we're ready," she said with a laugh.

"Yeah, I'm coming."

I hung up and went to my bunk for my clothes. When I got to the showers, Megan was already under a showerhead. She pointed to the closest one on the back wall as Danielle walked up to the shower head next to her. We talked the entire time, just laughing and goofing off. Thank god I wasn't shy about my body being seen, because literally anyone could see you showering, including the guard. It was uncomfortable, but Megan and Danielle had me laughing so much I barely noticed the other women watching us. Once we were done, we dried off in front of the sinks and put our clothes on.

"Don't worry about the wandering eyes during your first week," Megan said. "They like to shower stalk all the new bodies."

Nine o'clock rolled around, and the guard turned off the lights over the bunks. I lay down and pulled my Buddhism book out to read myself to sleep. It felt good to have air conditioning again, and that made me sleep like a baby.

Chapter 11. Parish to Prison

My first morning in prison, I woke at 4 a.m. for morning chow. I couldn't imagine someone rolling chow trays all the way to the barracks or to the compound on the other side, so I knew we weren't eating in our pods. The guard stood up at the front table and announced that we would line up for chow in seven minutes. I got up to relieve my bladder, and as I walked back to my bunk I saw everyone putting their yellows on.

"Yellows must be worn in the cafeteria," the guard yelled at us.

I got to my bunk and I pulled my yellows on as I walked toward the chow line. The guard opened the door and pointed to the corner of the gate for us to line up at. We all walked up in a straight line, and the other pods in the barracks lined up behind us. We walked the long route to the cafeteria and then stood in line again at the door, waiting for a yellow badge to escort us in.

"Pull your pants up," the yellow badge said to the chick behind me as she walked up and grabbed the door. The girl pulled her pants up a smidge as the officer stared at her.

"You don't want to listen to me? Okay," she said, and walked out.

As the line moved toward the front, I scanned the big dining hall. There were tables that sat four all around, a kitchen in the back, and three inmates behind the counter ready to serve food. As we received our trays, one of the inmates serving us looked up at me and smiled. Glancing around, she threw an extra biscuit onto my tray and handed it to the next worker, gave it to me.

I followed the line and sat next to some women from my pod. As I looked over my tray, the same yellow badge walked back in carrying a yellow one-piece jumper. She threw it at the girl she'd told to pull her pants up.

"This is what you're wearing if you ever come into the cafeteria now," she yelled as she walked back to her post by the door.

Breakfast was steaming hot and fresh. I had eggs, sausage, grits, and two biscuits. Everything tasted good, like it was made from an actual buffet outside of the walls and locked gates. I demolished my entire tray.

"Let's go, ladies," a guard yelled at us. I looked up and saw that most of the tables were full and women were still lining up outside. The guards rushed us, and the tables in front of me started shoving their food down their throats before standing up to dump their trays and leave. I was eating pretty fast already, so it didn't take me long to finish up. I walked out with my belly fuller than it had ever been from incarcerated food and waited with the rest of the women who'd finished. We had to stand outside the cafeteria until the whole barracks had finished before we could all head back to the pods. It was around five in the morning and early November, so it was about 65 degrees in northern Louisiana, and we had no jackets unless we'd brought one into prison. I rushed inside Foxtrot as soon as the guards unlocked the pods. It was still early, so I lay back down and went back to sleep.

"Yard," I heard a guard. I open my eyes to movement all around. Everyone was getting dressed, putting on makeup, doing their hair, and brushing their teeth. It didn't take much for me to get ready. I just threw on my yellows and walked outside, following the crowd into the yard. On the way, I heard my name being called. I turned around to see Amy running toward me for a hug, her girlfriend trailing right behind.

I was kind of relieved to walk to the yard with people I knew. As we entered together, we saw women all over, some playing basketball with a flat ball and no net, some playing volleyball at a net set up in the grass, and some just loitering around the walkways. We found a spot in the grass to stand around and chat. I saw women walking like they were on the track, except they were in the grass, creating a little dirt trail with their feet.

About an hour passed, and we started to walk back toward the barracks. The people who'd stayed in the barracks had created their own yard around the pods, inside our gated area, so most of the women in the barracks didn't go to the big yard.

On the other side of the grass in the compound, there were three big buildings named Louisiana, Kansas, and Michigan. The Michigan pod was in the middle of the yard, in the same building as the infirmary. I'd heard that Kansas and Louisiana had two-man cells and a bigger day room. Those pods were closer to the commissary store and the barbershop, which was inside the commissary building. On the walkway to Louisiana and Kansas, you passed the library right before you come to a gated pavilion. That was used for church events and other random things, but mainly inmates went to the back room of the pavilion, where there was an ice maker, and they would fill up ice chests and bring them back to the pods to share ice. The infirmary also had a window like a drive-thru pharmacy, except it was run by an officer and you weren't in a car. Inmates lined up at that window during the three medicine calls. Rain, shine, sleet, hail, or hurricane, you had to stand in line if you wanted your medicine. And you had to show the guard that you'd swallowed it. "Open wide, stick your tongue out, move your tongue up and down," the guards would instruct.

I returned with Amy and her girlfriend. They stayed in the pod next door to mine. As I walked in, I heard the guard yell for commissary sheets. I ran to my bunk and hurried to fill my sheet out. Not only did you have to check off everything you wanted, you also had to add up your own total, and there were no calculators or kiosks to check the balance on your books. I checked off saltine crackers, some new clothes like socks, boxers, and t-shirts, and my seafood. I thought I only had fifty dollars transferred from the parish when I was shipped. I put my commissary sheet on top of the rest that were placed at the front table, and the guard stopped me before I could walk away.

"Take the stack to the canteen building," she ordered me.

I grabbed the stack and headed for the door. I didn't know my way around yet, but I didn't really care—anything was better than hearing forty loud voices.

As I took my lonely walk across the prison yard, I noticed how empty it looked when everyone was confined to their pods. I took the long walkway toward the canteen building. All I knew was that the building was past the compound, so I kept walking. As I got close to the library, Amy walked out, and we almost ran into each other. Her eyes were damp.

"Amy, you okay?"

"No, man. My girlfriend is being shipped to a rehab facility." She started to tear up, so I tried to calm her.

"Well, isn't that a good thing? She gets to get out of here."

"To be honest, I think I'm sadder that I just know I'll never hear from her again." She started to cry.

"Why wouldn't you hear from her?" I asked in confusion.

"Because she looked at me as a joce. As soon as she found out she was accepted to a rehab facility, she started talking about her boyfriend, and what she was going to do with herself once she was out. She didn't say anything about writing me or even talking to me."

"Hey! Y'all need to keep walking and get where you need to be before I give y'all bed confinement!" We looked up and saw a guard walking toward us from the barracks as she yelled. We rolled our eyes.

"We'll catch up later." Amy wiped her eyes and started back to the barracks.

I continued on to the canteen building. When I knocked on the door, a Mexican woman opened it and watched me with big eyes as I walked in.

"I came to bring these sheets." I handed her the stack of papers.

"You're so cute. This must be your first commissary, because I would have noticed you," she said as she scanned me from top to bottom. She took the stack and asked me for my name as she shuffled through the commissary sheets.

"Mercedes," I told her.

"Okay, Mercedes. Well, thanks for the drop. We'll call Foxtrot as soon as we fix the orders." She winked and closed the door behind me.

I took my time walking back to enjoy the sunlight and the breeze. I saw couples who'd snuck out of their dorms to get some alone time with one another. There were a few blind spots around the yard and compound. For instance, the library had a wall by the entrance that you could lean against and not be seen. There was also a spot by the doors to Kansas and Louisiana that hid bodies well enough. The most popular spot was in the hallway of the infirmary and Michigan. Every blind spot I passed had a couple in it until I reached the walkway to the barracks and cafeteria.

As I passed the dining hall, I smelled smoke in the air. Closer to the barrack pods, it got stronger. I hit the corner of the walkway where it intercepted the shortcut to the compound, to which the gate was usually locked, and then turned toward the barracks. There was a tiny, one-person shed there with a window. It looked like a place for a traffic conductor to rest, but since this was a prison I assumed it was just a spot that the guards used to use to stand watch. From beaten-down the little shed was, you could tell it was no longer in use. As I get closer, I saw smoke rising out of it. Two inmates were inside, ducking down as they passed a joint back and forth. I walked past, and they watched me.

"You wanna hit?"

"No, I'm good," I replied, not even knowing what they were smoking.

As I get closer to where the walkway split left and right to the pods, I saw a guard walking out of Echo pod toward the shed.

"*Cuckoo, cuckoo! I hear the birds flocking,*" I sang loud enough for the two inmates to hear as I continued on. I heard the shed door open and close as I passed the guard. I turned back and saw the two inmates turn the corner, coming in the direction I was. Looking paranoid, they walked faster to catch up with me.

"Thanks for the heads-up," one of them told me.

"Just looking out," I told her back.

"Well, I work in the cafeteria, so next time I see you, I'll have something for you," she told me as they walked into the Alpha pod. I nodded as I continued to Foxtrot.

Inside the pod, women were putting on their yellows. *Must be close to chow.* I did like the rest of them and then sat at the table where the guard was, along with Danielle and Megan. When chow was called, we walked to the dining hall together, as we usually ate together. We skipped the line, another normal routine, and got inside to be next in line for trays. The inmate handing me my tray slipped a folded-up piece of paper underneath it and eyeballed me to grab it. I took both and went to my table, and as I sat down, I put the paper into my sock.

"I saw that. I'll ask to read it later," Danielle said as she stuffs her mouth with chicken and okra. I laughed and started to stuff my mouth as well.

We rushed out as soon as we finished and headed toward the locked gates to sit and wait for everyone else. I took out the note and opened it up.

"I think your so cute and I would like to get to know you a little better. Write me back if your interested." I balled it up and tossed it to the ground.

Danielle picked it up and read it, then looked up at me. "Ohhh, you got your first dike kite! Why'd you throw it? She works in the cafeteria. We could get some extra food out of her." She laughed and shoved me playfully.

"She's illiterate. If you don't know the difference between *your* and you're, then you don't need to be writing letters to people," I joked back. It was really to avoid having women think I was interested in them while I had a girlfriend at home. The compliments were nice, but I learned in the parish that jail relationships started quickly and the drama escalated even faster, and that was a huge turn-off for me. It was an even bigger turn-off to see how much more protective people were, and how much more drama took place among the prison couples. I witnessed a stud who had a full beard and mustache go off on another stud just for asking their girlfriend for a packet of ketchup. I stayed as far as I could from unnecessary drama.

Later that evening, as I was sitting at the front table putting my puzzle together, the guard interrupted my activity and asked me to go get ice. Normally, I would jump up and run in my excitement to be out of the pod while everyone was housed, but I really didn't feel like walking far in the cold weather.

As I rolled the cooler onto the walkway toward the pavilion, I saw someone getting ice for the pod next door. It was Amy.

"Wait for me," she yelled.

We walked the long walk together and talked about things we'd never known about each other. We would always joke and laugh about things that were happening in front of us, but we never actually knew about each other's lives outside the gates. Eventually, she interrupted the life conversation with "My girlfriend was shipped earlier."

I looked at her, wondering what I was supposed to say or how to comfort her. I was never good at that. So I tried to make her laugh instead. "At least you don't have to share your commissary anymore."

She did laugh. "Well, she was the one who carried that heavy laundry bag to the barracks for me."

"I'll carry it for you. It's not that heavy," I told her, hoping I'd made her feel better.

She stopped walking for a second to look me in

my eyes and said she would like that. It was the first time I actually looked at her features. Amy had big, pretty blue eyes, straight teeth that complimented her smile, short-brown hair, and a big booty with wide hips for a white girl. We turned back to finish our walk, passing couples in the blind spots who made it awkward. We walked slower than the other ice runners so we could talk a little longer. It seemed like the conversation would never end, but it had to when we reached our pods.

"Well, I guess I'll see you for chow tomorrow," she said, giving me a hug that lasted longer than normal. We separated and went inside.

After I called Diamond, and got none of the love I wanted or expected. I lay down to sleep.

All the dorm lights flick on at once.

"*Everyone get up! It's a shake-down!*" There was one yellow badge who was higher ranked than the others, and she was the definition of a bitter bitch. I'd tried to make her laugh, and sometimes it worked, but other times she'd just give me a "get the fuck out of my face" look. Inmates always tried to stay on her good side because she had the authority to threw you in the hole, assign bed confinement, or even write you up to add time to your sentence.

"I'm tired of getting complaints about people stealing other people's shit, so here's my solution. Everyone sit in the day room," she ordered us.

We got up slowly and angrily, complaining as we walked to the tables to sit down to see what was going to happen. The yellow badge started at the bunks opposite the door, instructing the other guards to help. She went to the first bunk and threw the mat off, tossed all the papers that were under it to the ground, and opened the duffle bag that was underneath the bunk and flipped it upside-down, spilling everything onto the floor.

"Fall in! I want everything out of bags and drawers and onto the floor. Skip nothing!"

The other guards started tossing everyone's belongings into piles in the little spaces between the bunks. They even poured all the liquids out of the bottles, so that the piles were drenched too. When they were done, you couldn't even see the cold concrete floor anymore. The dorm looked as though a tornado had run through it a half-dozen times.

"Now, I want this pod spotless before y'all can have lights-out," the yellow badge yelled as she and her minions walked out of the dorm.

Inmates hurried to their bunks, stepping over and on all the stuff on the floor.

"They spilled my pickle juice all over my clothes, man!"

I heard everyone complaining and crying. Some people had had their photos ripped or drenched in soda that the guards had poured out. Photos and mail were scattered across the room. It was like a game of finders-keepers, where you had to move quickly to spot your things and snatch them up before someone else could. Most the inmates were sad about soaked and torn family photos. Some couldn't find their photos and letters at all.

The guards had even put all our mats and pillows in a stack, so we had to try to recognize our own while they all looked basically the same. I'd had my pillow wrapped in my sheet, but I'd seen a guard take the sheet off as she threw the mat and pillow into the pile with the others. So I kept my eyes on them the whole time. I grabbed my mat and pillow first, thanking god that I was close to a back corner. Most of my stuff had ended up in one place, close to my bunk. I managed to clean up my bunk area while the rest of the dorm still looked like the aftermath of a soda tsunami.

After we'd picked everything up off the floors, the orderly mopped up the soda, pickle juice, and random food splatters. By the time we finished, the guards were calling for breakfast chow. We all lay down exhausted and skipped the meal.

Chapter 12. No Soft Sides

"Yard is over," the guards yelled.

I started slowly toward the back, where the barracks were. When yard is over, everyone takes their time getting back to their pods. It's like trying to end a party where nobody wants to go home. As I took the long route, I saw a group of women who I knew were supposed to be going the opposite way, as they'd stayed in the compound. They were acting suspicious, looking over their shoulders and whispering. As I got close, I heard a familiar voice.

"Cedes!" Red walked out of the group. "Was a yellow badge following you this way?"

"Nah, they were all walking to the compound," I informed her.

"Ok, good. It's time, y'all." She started toward the laundry room door that was connected to the cafeteria. "You want a show?" she asked me, turning back. "A fight's about to go down in the laundry room, for like three minutes."

Fights were one of the things I enjoyed the most, so I nodded and followed.

Inside the laundry room, it was pretty obvious who was about to fight. It was a thick, dark-skinned chick and a tall, light-skinned chick. They wasted no time, both fighters taking their shirts off and throwing their sets up. The fight started in less than thirty seconds and, with a head hanging out the door as a lookout, it continued for two minutes. The fight was fair until the light-skinned chick stumbled and her opponent managed to top her. *She's done for,* I thought. Then someone in the audience threw a sock full of rocks directly in front of the light-skinned one. She picked it up swung it at the other girl's head.

Crack!

The dark-skinned chick started fumbling with her weight, trying to stand up, and the light-skinned one quickly stood and swung at her face again. It sounded like a car crash every time the sock made contact with the girl's face, and I winced at the sound.

"Yellow! Yellow!" the lookout called.

"Flake!" Red screamed, and headed for the door.

As I followed her out, I turned back to see the fighters hurrying to get their yellow tops on. The dark-skinned girl could barely open her eyes, and she was the last to make it out of the door. A yellow badge walking toward the cafeteria told us to go to our pods and continued on. Everyone scattered for their bunks, and I looked back one more time to see that the dark-skinned chick couldn't open her eyes, and her mouth was leaking blood. I wondered if she would take herself to the infirmary or just tough it out. Anyone who went to the infirmary with bad injuries was investigated, meaning you'd be considered a snitch afterward.

I reached the Foxtrot pod in a crowd of other women. As the guards started to lock down the gates so that no inmates could enter or exit the barracks area, I heard a vehicle riding over rocks close by. I look toward the noise and I saw the white van approaching the intake building. *Must be a new shipment.*

"Everyone in their pods," the guards yelled outside all the doors. I walked in just as the sun was going down.

"You wanna go to church tonight?" Megan asked me when I got in.

"Church? Since when do you go to church?" I responded, making a face.

She rolled her eyes in embarrassment. "I'm meeting someone there and I don't wanna go alone. Everyone in church is joced out, I need that right now," she explained.

"Sure, not like I have anything better to do," I told her.

"Good! We have to have our yellows on, and we need to be the first five in line, because the yellow badge tonight only allows five women from each pod to go."

"Well, you better hold my spot when you get yours." I shoved her and laughed.

As I walked to my bunk to lay out my yellows for the night, the pod door opened and two new women walked in with mats. It was a little late for newcomers, but it was prison. Everything was unpredictable. I remember the empty bunk above me and prepared to accept a new being living on top of me.

The two women were complete opposites. One was short and caramel-colored with short, curly hair. The other was a tall Caucasian lady with long, brown hair. She looked like she played softball or basketball. The caramel girl walked toward my row. I assumed that was my new bunkie, and I walked behind her so I could gather the belongings I had on the top bunk.

"You moving into this bunk?" I asked her.

"Yeah, you're under me?" she turned to ask me.

"Yeah. I have some of my clothes on it, though, I'll grab them real quick." As I moved my clean clothes, my new bunkie undressed completely. I turned my head to avoid looking at her naked body.

"Um, are you getting dressed for the club or something?" I asked without looking.

"No, I'm going to shower. The ride here was long as hell," she responded nonchalantly. "Do you have an extra towel? Mine hasn't come back from the wash yet."

I never let people borrow my stuff, in or out of jail. "No, but the lady to our right might have some," I responded as I walked away from the naked human. I sat down at a table with Danielle and Megan.

"Damn, your new bunkie is fine as hell," Danielle said as she watched the newbie walk to the shower.

"Looks like everyone agrees," Megan laughed. As we watched, a crowd of women circled around the showers to get a better view of the new bodies in the pod. My new bunkie was something to admire, especially around a lot of women who didn't have all their front teeth or hair.

"What's your name?" someone yelled while she was cleaning herself.

"Misha," she replied without stopping.

Misha had a small waist to complement her wide hips, a pretty smile, and curly hair that she kept in a high bun. She was also nowhere close to shy. She walked out of the shower still dripping water and went straight to our bunks like she was walking a runway, except she wasn't modeling clothes, she was modeling soapy water. All eyes still on her, she took her time drying off and putting her clothes on.

"It's time to line up for church," the guard yelled out.

Megan, already sitting closest to the door, stood up and started the line. "I have the first two slots," she yelled to the crowd who were walking up. A few women got mad, but they quickly went back to their business.

"Where are y'all going?" Danielle asked us.

"Megan wants to go girlfriend hunting," I laughed.

"I got third slot. I don't care what y'all gotta say about it," Danielle yelled.

The third lady in line claimed the fourth slot, and the folks behind her started arguing with one another about who would take the last. There were more older women than younger ones in the pod, so we never had a problem getting our way. As we lined up to leave, I hurried back to my bunk to put my yellows on. Misha was still half-naked, applying lotion and other hygiene products. I stood on the opposite side of her naked body as I changed into my yellow suit. As I took my pants off, I saw her staring at me with those big, brown eyes. She winked, still half-naked, so I quickly put the rest of my clothes on and rejoined the line.

We walked slowly to the classroom building. We were the last group, so all the chairs inside were taken and we had to sit on the floor. A woman and a man stood at the podium with a microphone. This was supposed to be a church service, but it was more one of those "I've found my purpose" types of speeches.

"We came for the food," Megan turned and told one of her friends from the compound.

Church services and other random events that took place in the classroom or the pavilion were the only times the barracks' women were mixed in with the compound women. Anyone in the barracks who had a girlfriend from the compound used the opportunity as a date night. Depending on which yellow badge was in charge of the services, you might have a good date. If it was a mean yellow badge, and they knew two women were a couple, they would try their hardest to keep them separated or even kick one of them out. Most couples didn't care, though. They were too worried about being with their girlfriends. If you had a lot of time on your sentence, it was the best way to make it go by faster.

After the service, the woman and man handed us candy on our way out the door. That was probably the best part of the night. We took extra long walking back to the barracks, since we took a detour to the compound to see some friends. When we got back to Foxtrot, I went straight to my bunk and fell asleep.

The next morning I found myself standing back to back with other women at the phones and listening to the automated lady's voice explaining how phone calls were recorded and whatnot, I waited patiently for Diamond to answer. She usually picked up within the second ring, but lately she'd been answering after about five. I could normally hear her pressing buttons over the voice asking if you would accept the call. It was about eight o'clock at night, and the phones were shut off at nine except on weekends, when they didn't shut them off until ten. Two missed calls later, I tried again. I was thinking the worst when she finally picked up the phone.

"Hello," she said in an annoyed voice.

"What's up? Are you okay?" I asked her frantically.

"I'm fine, what's up?" she replied, as if everything was normal.

"Um, why didn't you answer? Are you busy? You never ignore my calls," I said in a confused manner.

"I didn't ignore your call, I never got it. I'm at home watching television," she answered, fast.

It was quiet on the phone for a second. *Ring. Ring.* I heard a phone in the background.

"You sure you're at home?" I asked, all concerned.

"Yes! I'm at home. You're hearing the television," she yelled back.

I got quiet again. I heard the things she was telling me, but my body was getting mixed signals from my brain. *She's with someone. She's definitely not at home.* I tried to ignore it and just changed the subject.

"So how was your day? Did you go to work?" I asked, hoping to improve the mood.

"Yes, and it was okay." She sounded like I was interrupting whatever she was doing. My body started to get warm inside, and my heart started racing as I listened to the background hard to find the answers that she wasn't giving. Then I heard a deep voice.

"Who was that?" I asked, still trying to be calm.

"Nobody. That's the television. You don't trust me? What's your problem?" she asked.

"I don't have a problem. Things just don't feel right. You know you can tell me anything, right? If you're lonely, I understand," I told her, knowing deep down that I would be hurt, but I would deal with it when I got home.

"I'm not with anyone, Cedes! I'll call you back." Before I could ask what number she was going to dial, because we both knew she couldn't call me back, she hung up and I was left with the dial tone.

She's going to call me back? Why would she lie to me? I was in prison, what could I do if she told me the truth? Leave? Was she trying to get revenge on me for being with Jaylon in the parish? My mind was too cluttered. I put the phone down and I headed to my bunk and started writing down everything that was on my mind.

An hour later, I found myself with five pages covered front and back with ink. I did feel a little better, but I still needed answers. My right-side neighbor was looking at me.

"You okay? You working on a series of novels over there?" she chuckled.

"Yeah, I'm good," I responded, still writing and never taking my eyes off the paper.

Danielle walked up to the corner by my bunk. "Everything good?"

It was too obvious when anyone had an issue. Being around the same people every second of the day, you started noticing every change in behavior or mood. Stepping off of the phone and going straight to your bunk was a big tip-off.

"Yeah, I'm okay. Just trying to piece together a puzzle," I coded for her.

She caught on to my desire for privacy and knelt down closer. "Was it your girlfriend?"

I nodded. After I gave her a brief account of what I'd just heard, she stood up and scratched her head.

"Maybe she's working too much, and it's just overwhelming not having you home with her, paying bills by herself and whatnot," she said, trying to calm me down.

I tried to add other scenarios to my brain so it could stop overthinking, but it was tough. I didn't call Diamond back until the next morning. She seemed normal again, but lately I'd started feeling a different vibe from her even through the prison phones. We'd been six hours apart for three months now, but it had started to feel even more distant. Our conversations had grown shorter. We'd stopped talking about how it would be once I got out, and it seemed like we were just wasting bought minutes on the phone. I started to call her less often through the day to see if she would sound more excited to hear my voice, but it didn't change anything. It actually made it worse for me. I'd miss her and think of her way more than normal, and then my heart would drop when I finally called her and heard her unexcited voice. I felt like a kid going to a carnival but not being allowed to ride anything. I kept wondering if she even loved me anymore, or if this rollercoaster was just too much for her to handle. I'd saved up about three months of bill money for her before going back to jail to take away from her responsibilities while I was gone. I just couldn't piece together why she was acting so differently.

As much as I wanted to cry myself to sleep, there were way too many eyes and ears in the room for that kind of scene. I had to keep it tough. Diamond's birthday was coming up, and it hurt me not to be there for her. But that wouldn't stop me from going out of my way to impress her.

I gave my dad a call. "Diamond's birthday is a week from now. Do you mind sending flowers to her job from me?" My dad lived about two hours from Diamond.

"Of course I can," he responded. After we talked about the lawyer, saying the same things over and over, I hung up and wasted more time on the thousand-piece puzzle I'd started on the front-row table. Troubled by my relationship, I started overthinking things even more. Most of the day, I wrote letters to my family and Diamond, then I slept until dinner chow. They were serving meat and rice, so I decided to eat something from my commissary. As most of the women went out, I was left in the pod with just my left-bottom bunk neighbor and the guard. I sat on my bed and pulled my duffle bag out from underneath it. My neighbor, I heard people call her Jaz, turned to me with a bowl in her hand.

"Not fucking with that stew today?"

"Nah, I'd rather eat my oysters and crackers."

"That's what I'm eating too," she laughed.

As I put an oyster onto a saltine, she laughed out loud.

"You okay?" I asked in confusion.

"Man, you not doing it right at all." She reached for my bowl. "I'm about to show you something you gonna do every time you eat oysters out of the bag." She pulled out bottles of sriracha sauce, Worcestershire sauce, mustard, and hot sauce, adding a bit of everything to the oysters and then stirring them around before handing the bowl back to me.

"Dip a chip now," she said with a smile of satisfaction.

I looked worriedly down at the slop, but I grabbed a cracker, picked up an oyster with it, and threw it into my mouth. She was right. I was amazed, and never eating oysters and crackers the same way again. It was so good I started eating it every night. I even got my own bottles of sriracha, mustard, Worcestershire, and hot sauce the next time I ordered oysters off the commissary.

Full from the new recipe, when all the women were back from chow I took my group shower with Danielle and Megan as usual. I noticed Misha following me to the showers while I was undressing.

"So I see you have a shower stalker," Danielle said, and Megan laughed. I turned toward the day room and saw Misha sitting at the table closest to the sinks. It wasn't hard to notice—if you weren't back there to take an actual shower or use the sinks, you were obviously stalking someone.

After making eye contact, she winked and walked away. I finished up my shower, dried off, and pulled my nightclothes on. I went through my normal nighttime routine, listening to my radio while playing spades, calling my parents, and finally calling Diamond, who seemed to have shorter conversations with me every night. Then I went to lie down and write letters to my friends outside the locked fences. As I got sleepy, I put my writing tablet away, lay back on top of my pillow, and set my radio up where I could get a signal. Relaxed, I closed my eyes to finish another day in this shit hole.

When I was in a deep sleep, I felt something pulling at my shorts. I jumped up in a second and saw Misha kneeling beside my bunk with her hands on my shorts, which were halfway down my legs. My first reaction was a fist to her jaw.

Misha fell back and grabbed her face. She staggered up and looked down at me with evil eyes. I turned toward the guard to make sure she didn't hear anything so we wouldn't create a scene, then I pulled my shorts up and looked back at Misha with eyes that would kill. Without a word, she climbed back up to her bunk. I fell back asleep with one eye open.

I slept through morning chow and woke up a few

minutes before lunch. The dorm doors were open, which meant people were moving in or out. Today, it was both. A little old black woman with no teeth or hair walked in with her green mat and a bag of commissary items. As I watched to see which bunk she walked to, I saw Misha packing her bags before walking towards the pod door. She glanced back at me and after rolling her eyes, she walks out of the pod. The old woman was then placed in the bunk on the right-side of me.

The guard told us we couldn't leave, so some of us just stood in the doorway to watch the show of people moving. Next door, two women with mats walked out excitedly, saying they were moving into the compound. I was kind of mad that I wasn't on the moving list. I was tired of being in the barracks, where new intakes were in and out like mosquitos. The women in the compound had been sentenced already and were just sitting, waiting for their time to go home. The barracks were more like a holding cell for people who could still bond out, awaiting for trial or transfer to another facility. Another body with a mat came out of the pod next door, and I saw that it was Amy.

"Cedes! You weren't on the moving list? How? We've been here the same amount of time." She looked around, all confused.

"I'm not understanding either. I'm so ready to move out of here," I responded. The disappointment was clear in my voice.

"They have me moving to Kansas. I won't be able to hit the ice run with you anymore," she said, making a sad face.

"I'll see you during yard, I promise!" Watching Amy struggle with her duffle bag, laundry bag, and mat, I walked out of the pod to help her carry her stuff.

"Cedes, get back in your pod," the Foxtrot guard said without even getting up.

"I'm going help some of the inmates move," I yelled back at her as I continued to walk with Amy's bag over my shoulder. We talked as we make the long trip to the compound, walking slowly the entire way to waste time. When we finally got to the door of Kansas, the guards in the tower saw us and popped the door open. I walked in behind Amy and scanned the new scenery. There was a glass tower in the middle of the unit, like the one in the parish jail, and four doors leading to different pods. There were windows in the walls separating the tower courtyard from the four pods. You could see right into the day rooms of the pods and the stairs that led to more cells. The showers were in the front, in the corner by the windows. They were like the ones at the parish jail, minus shower curtains. Concrete walls separated the three showerheads, and in front of the showers was a half-wall to hang your towel and clean clothes on.

The guard in the tower asked if I was moving in, and after I told her no, she waved for me to exit. As I walked out, I saw some other women struggling with their bags and offered to help them into the Louisiana unit. That pod had the same set up as Kansas, but for some reason it seemed a little dirtier and darker.

I finally walked back toward my own pod in the barracks, until I ran into Megan with her bag of commissary and her mat.

"What the fuck? I know you're not being moved too," I said angrily.

She dropped her stuff and gave me a big hug. "I need for you to get on that moving list, man," she said sadly. "I'm going to miss you. They're housing me in Michigan, so I won't be too far."

"Nah, be happy, man. You're getting out of these dirty-ass barracks. I'll help you carry your bags down to Michigan, though," I offered.

"Hell yeah! Come see my new roommates with me," she said excitedly.

We started the long walk from the barracks, passing the dining room/laundry room and following the zigzagging fences that led to the compound. In Michigan pod, Megan's bunk was in the middle of a row. The pod was just a slightly bigger version of the barrack pods. There were still forty women in one room, but their day room had an area for the television and couch, and the tables were in the middle between the living area and the row of bunks. I put Megan's commissary bag under her bunk and told her that I'd see her for chow or during yard. We never had a distinct time for yards. It was just whenever the yellow badges were in a good enough mood to call for it. As I headed out of Michigan to go back to the barracks, I heard a familiar voice.

"Cedes?"

I turned around right before I hit the door and found myself face to face with Jaylon. She gave me that smile that always made me smile with her, and she came over and gave me a big hug.

She was a little thicker since the parish. I

assumed it came from the fact that they were serving food that was actually worth eating. All the old feelings started rushing back to me, but there was something a little off about her energy. I turned back to the door, since the guard was staring at me and waving me on.

Back at Foxtrot, I went straight to my bunk. I was already sad and bored without Megan. I still had Danielle, but she was sadder than I was, so she slept most of the day. I followed the same routine and napped a lot more.

One morning, I didn't wake up for 4 a.m. chow. I'd fallen asleep with my radio in my ears so I wouldn't be woken up by all the movements in the dorm. Instead, I woke up on my own around ten and called Diamond. She told me to call her back later because she was busy. *She's never done that before. She always says hang on if she's at work or her hands are tied.* I started letting my imagination run wild.

"Damn, that was a short call. Your girlfriend mad at you?"

I turned to see a white chick sitting up in her bunk. *Ear hustlers*, I thought as I rolled my eyes. I hated how small and crowded the pod was. If your bunk was closest to the three phones, you could literally hear everyone's conversations.

I walked away from the phones to work on my puzzle up front. A yellow badge walked in quickly with Misha by her side and talked to the guard, then left. Five minutes later, the guard walked Misha to her bunk and grabbed her mat, then threw it on top of an empty bunk two rows to the right of mine. I smiled a little, now that the drama had moved down the room. I was perfectly fine with that.

About eight hours later, I tried to call Diamond again. She told me she was busy again, and that I should just call tomorrow. *What the fuck. I barely spoke to her all day, and she doesn't seem bothered by that the way I am.*

"She's cheating, honey. Sorry to have to say it." That was another lady whose bunk was too close to the phones.

"You don't know the situation. Thanks for being nosey, though," I snarled back.

I went to bed mad as hell, feeling like you'd see fire if you looked in my pupils. I got to my bunk and started a letter to Diamond, but I balled it up. It was just venting, and I knew she wouldn't write back if I sent it. After that, I lay back on my bunk and waited to fall asleep.

I heard some noises like a bag of chips and looked around to see who was eating at this time, but I didn't see anybody awake. Since the shakedown, rats and mice had been bad in our pod. We had rat traps, but they were just the sticky pads. When they caught a mouse, it would still be alive, and we'd have to kill it.

The noise got louder and woke up the old lady next to me. She started checking her stuff and then screamed as a mouse took off from out of her little drawer toward the back wall. I just watched it run. I was used to seeing them running around at night, and having a duffle bag without holes and with a lock, they couldn't really get to my stuff. The old lady picked up a pack of noodles from her stash and looked at it. I could see the big circular hole in the package and in the actual slab of noodles. She got up to throw it away and then started looking for another place to put the rest of her commissary.

When she noticed I was awake, she asked "Could I put my food in your duffle?"

"No," I said, turning away in my bunk. I wasn't trying to be mean, but once you let one person do something, the other forty women will ask for the same deal. I wasn't going to be the babysitter of the pod.

By the morning of Diamond's birthday, I still hadn't called her back since she was so busy with whatever was going on outside the gates. I went to the phones and gave her a ring. It was about 11 a.m., and I knew that my dad had sent the flowers to her job by 9:30.

"Hello," Diamond answered.

"Happy birthday, baby. Did you get my gift?"

"Yes, they're beautiful. How did you do it?" she asked. I could hear by the background that she was around her coworkers.

"You know I will make ways for you, my love. I'm just really sorry I can't be there to celebrate with you and make it a better birthday." I tried to hold back my tears.

"It's okay, I still lo—"

"Happy birthday, baby." I heard another voice in the background.

"Who was that?" My eyebrows started to wrinkle up.

"It's nobody," she said quickly. I could hear her closing doors in the background.

"Who sent you these flowers?" It was the same voice, more lightly, like someone shouting through a closed door.

"I'm busy at work. Call me back later, baby. I love you," Diamond said, hanging up before I could respond. *They were right. She's with someone else.* I didn't know what else to do on my end. Every time something didn't feel right, I would write about it instead of telling anyone. As soon as the inmates had a fresh story to tell, it spread through the prison like a wildfire. I always kept my business to myself while everyone else told me theirs.

"Cedes!" someone yelled. I shook myself out of my thoughts. "Someone at the door for you!"

As I passed the guard, she warned me "Don't go out those gates."

We weren't even suppose to be outside, but this was a run-over guard we barely listened to. I open the door and faced Amy.

"How are you even back here?" I laughed and stepped out to the walkway.

"I got out for class, but they cancelled it. Thought I'd waste dorm time and pass by," she laughed.

I was impressed at her violating rules just to see me. We sat on the bench and joked around for an hour or so, until we saw a yellow badge walking out of the gates by the infirmary.

"Oops, that's my cue." She stood up and gave me a hug and then started back toward the compound. Time went by so fast whenever I was around her. I walked back inside before the yellow guard reached the barracks and went to my bunk to continue my letter, which I would also most likely not mail, since it was just me expressing my feelings. She never wrote back to that type of letter, so I would just write them and keep them to myself.

I gave Diamond a call that night to check on her and see if anything had changed in her attitude toward me.

"Hello. So I heard you called your dad before me," she barked through the phone.

"Wait, what?" I asked in confusion.

"You told your dad to come by the house? He popped up here while I was at work," she yelled.

"Um, I haven't called my dad today. I was going to call him as soon as I told you goodnight," I said. My eyebrows started to wrinkle up, and my chest started to tighten. "Why do you sound so guilty?"

"I'm not guilty. But he might explain the story from a different perspective," she said. "I was at work, and my friend needed to stay somewhere for a second, so I let him stay in the guest room. Your dad popped by the house and saw my friend." I waited, listening for a description of this friend, but instead she made me ask.

"Who is this friend?"

She told me I didn't know him, he was a friend from work. My face turned as red as a firetruck. *She's been having someone stay under our roof without telling me?* I hung up the phone. I'd never hung up in her face before, but I had to gather my thoughts before I called my dad.

"Hello?"

"What's up?" I asked in a shaky voice.

He noticed my tone and got right to the issue. "You talked to Diamond, huh? All I'm going to tell is what I saw." He waited for me to respond.

"Is she cheating on me?" I asked him.

"I don't know that answer, but I walked in and there was a tall, dark-skinned guy in a room with what looked like his bags of clothes," he said. "I passed by to drop mail that had your name on it."

"Okay," I said without expression. I had about a million things running through my mind. *Is that the reason she's been acting this way to me?* I was getting frustrated about not being able to do anything or talk to anyone face to face. After we hung up, I went to my bunk and started another letter to Diamond. I was definitely venting, as I wrote it fast and sloppy from the anger running through my body. *Why was there a random guy sleeping under the same roof as her?* After writing down my feelings, instead of letting the ear hustlers near the phone get my story and tell it to the compound like a newspaper, I finally calmed down enough to fall asleep.

Chapter 13. Joke's Up or Joce Up?

I started to lose interest in writing or calling Diamond as I hung out in the yard more or violated pod time to sneak into the compound and see Megan, Red, and Amy. There was no one I really spoke to in Foxtrot anymore besides Danielle who slept most of the time. Every chance I got to leave the pod, I took it. Whether it was getting ice or dropping off commissary sheets, I was the first one out the door. One day I went out for the afternoon ice run, hoping to run into Megan or Amy and speak with a familiar face, but I went a little too early and ended up being the only one out for ice. I got tired of walking around the compound waiting for others to come out, so I finally headed back to the barracks.

"Cedes!"

I turned around and saw Amy running toward me with her arms wide open.

"I was hoping to catch you before you went back in. I watched you from my dorm window but the guards wouldn't let me out to get the ice yet," she said as she gave me a long hug. For some reason the hug felt passionate, not like her usual hugs. "Would it be awkward for me to say that I missed you?" she asked, looking at me with those big, blue eyes.

"Why would it be awkward?" I smiled back, and her eyes lit up even more.

"I'll walk with you to the barracks."

She stayed close by my side, and we walked slowly, like we didn't want to leave each other. Along the way, we passed several inmates who complimented Amy on her appearance. "Damn, you're so pretty, and your ass is fat for a white girl," was what most of the compliments consisted of. Still, the more of them I heard, the more I started to look at Amy the same way the other inmates did. As I paid attention to her body and facial features, I did think that she was way too pretty to be in jail.

"You wanna turn around and walk the walkway again?" she asked me with a big grin.

I turned around and led the way back toward the pavilion. We both still had our ice chests rolling along behind us. We walked back and forth five or six times, until we saw a yellow badge walking toward the pavilion.

"Y'all get to your pods. Chow will be called in ten minutes," she said as she passed us.

Amy gave me another hug before going the opposite way. On my walk back to the barracks alone, I passed Michigan and caught Megan waving at me through the pod's small window. I waved back, knowing I wouldn't see her during chow. Then I came across four inmates standing around the laundry door. *Another blind spot.* I was dreading going back to the barracks, so I stood with the little group to see if the compound would be let out for chow first. As we waited, a woman from my pod came out of the laundry room.

"Aye, you going back to Foxtrot?" I yelled to her.

"Yeah, why?" She started, looking confused.

"This is the Foxtrot ice chest, could you take it with you? I forgot, I gotta run to the library," I lied.

"Yeah." She took the ice chest and started rolling it to Foxtrot while I remained in the blind spot. Luckily, the compound was let out first. I watched the crowd of inmates walking out of the pods from a distance, looking for Amy or Megan and any yellow badges or guards who might recognize me and make me go back to the barracks. Michigan was going to chow first, and I managed to meet up with Megan. I turned down her offer to go eat with her, though. I was anxious to find Red, and even more so to see Amy.

As I waited for the Michigan crew to finish leaving their dorms, Jaylon spotted me and gave me a big hug. "You eating chow with the compound today?" she asked me, looking over at the barracks.

"Yeah. I'm waiting for Kansas to get released."

Jaylon made a face and walked off. I turned back toward the other pods. Once all the Michigan inmates were in the chow line, Kansas was released. Their walk to the dining room was the longest. I spotted Amy from afar, since she was the only white girl with wide hips, which made her walk very distinctive. I didn't understand why my heart started racing and my excitement rose by a hundred percent. I felt like a kid about to open my gifts from Santa Claus.

When Amy finally hit the corner that had the straightaway to the dining hall. I walked halfway down to meet her. She gave me the biggest hug, almost jumped on top of me.

"How are you out right now? Barracks are eating last today." She shoved me with a smile.

"I saw some other folks sitting out, so I did too. I wanted to see you," I answered.

Her smile brightened the sky as she grabbed my arm and we walked toward the dining hall. We got in the chow line and started joking with each other.

"Y'all so cute together," a woman behind us said.

"Um, we're just friends. We were shipped together," I replied, and Amy nodded in agreement.

"Well shit, y'all might as well date. Y'all sexy as fuck standing by each other." She smiled and turned back to the conversation she was having with the lady behind her. Amy and I turned toward each other and laughed in unison.

We ate dinner together, and as we walked out of the dining hall, I noticed the gate to the barracks was locked. Amy noticed the same thing.

"Guess you're walking with me until the barracks are let out for chow," she said. She grabbed my arm and pulled me onto the walkway to the compound. We walked slowly, talking the whole time. We passed other couples who were walking slow to have more quality time with one another.

"Damn, we do look like a couple," I laughed, and pushed Amy away from me. I realized I hadn't seen Red yet, and most of the compound was walking back from the dining hall.

"Where's Red?" I asked Amy.

"I heard she went to the hole, but I don't know any details about why," she responded.

Damn, I miss my dawg. We got closer to Kansas, and I looked back to see if women were coming out of the barracks yet. They weren't.

"Let's turn around," Amy suggested. There were guards on most of the corners of the walkways, but they generally didn't care about couples or people wasting time getting back from chow. It was usually just the yellow badges who would force you back to your pod. Every guard we passed on our way back to the dining hall smiled or shook their head, like they knew something we didn't. The prison was so messy that most guards knew who were in relationships. As we walked extra slow past the classroom, we saw a yellow badge walking out of it.

"Oh, shit. I'm gonna turn around and head back. That yellow badge knows my ass, literally. She called my name once while my back was to her." Amy gave me a big hug and turned in the direction of Kansas. I walked to the locked gate and stood there as the yellow badge approached. *Shit, I'm gonna get written up.*

"Why are you out of the barracks? I know you're not from the compound, Cedes." The yellow badge looked around and then grinned at me. "You were talking to Amy, weren't you?"

"Yeah, we're from the same parish." I tried to keep her from thinking any further than a friendship between Amy and me.

"Okay. I won't fuss today, but you know better

than to violate like this. It's time for chow for the barracks anyway." She started unlocking the gate and called the dispatcher to release the barracks. I waited where I was for the other inmates to come out. Danielle usually managed to be the first one out so she could get to the front of the line.

"Cedes! Where the fuck you been?" she shouted from the other side of the walkway.

"I been saving your spot in line! You're welcome.

She laughed as she approached me. "Let's go eat," she said as she pulled her spork out of her bra.

We were first in line, so we went straight to the chow servers. "I won't tell anyone," the inmate handing out trays told me. You were definitely not allowed to eat twice, and if the dining hall workers noticed a double dipper, they were supposed to refuse them and let the authorities know. I took my tray with a slick grin and walked to the first table with Danielle. I only ate half of my food, though.

"You not hungry?" Danielle asked me around a full mouth.

"I ate with Amy," I told her.

Her eyes got wider than a cow's ass. "First of all, you left me? Second of all, Amy? What's up with that?" She looked at me with sexual eyes.

"Don't even think that far, we're just friends. I miss my parish people. And I have a girlfriend," I said in a serious tone.

"Okay, but your outside girlfriend has a new friend, so you could have you an inside friend. The math adds up," she joked.

We both laughed, even though deep down I knew she was right. I thought more about Amy as we got up and returned to the barracks.

"Aye, they have some kind of event going down Friday under the pavilion. We're going," Danielle ordered.

I nodded, because I attended anything that meant leaving the pods, except for the classes they offered to reduce your sentence by a month or two. You needed a two-year sentence or longer to be eligible for those. Most of them were eight months to a year long.

At Foxtrot, we took our showers and then I headed to the phones to check on Diamond.

"Hello? Cedes?" I heard Diamond ask.

"What's up, baby?" I said, excited to hear her voice.

"Why didn't you call this morning?"

"I figured I'd let you miss me," I replied. "Last few nights, your voice sounded like you weren't in the mood to talk to me. So, I gave you some *you* time."

"Well, I miss your voice, and definitely your face," she said in a sad tone.

Our conversation was actually decent that night, and we hung up on good terms. The next morning, I woke up for lunch chow, since we were first to eat. I followed Danielle to the front of the line again to eat. One of the dining room workers were one of the women who I saw smoking out of the little shack. Once she saw me in the chow line, I saw her throw extra spoonfuls of food onto my tray. "Well, that's unfair," Danielle laughed at me as she watched the extra full tray get handed to me. When we were done eating and walking back, I stopped near the end of the chow line.

"What are you doing?" Danielle turned around when she noticed I wasn't by her side anymore.

"You go on without me. I'm going to see if I can catch the compound folks." I waved for her to stop waiting, but she turned back and joined me at the end of the line.

"I wanna see my people, too," she said.

We chatted while we waited for the compound, and the chow line got shorter and shorter. Finally the barracks were done with, and we were the last ones remaining outside. We didn't see any yellow badges, so we waited in the blind spot by the laundry door. Finally, all three pods in the compound opened up and the inmates came rushing out.

We saw Megan first, since Michigan was closest to the dining hall. She hugged us both and started talking to Danielle while I kept looking out for Amy. When I saw her walking past the library, I started toward her, meeting her halfway and leaving my crew behind. We ended up eating chow together again, and then I walked her back to Kansas before returning to the barracks. I knew the strict yellow badge was on duty this morning, so I didn't risk getting into trouble. I got to Foxtrot and went straight to the table where my puzzle was.

As I started putting pieces together, a group of inmates sat down across from me. They started to move my puzzle around, and one of them knocked a piece off the table.

"Man, get the fuck from round my table," I said

in my deepest, angriest voice. Most of the pod already knew not to come around. My spot was at the end of the front table right under the television, so nobody really sat there, because you couldn't see the television. The guards always sat at the other end of the same table, right in front of the pod door. To get across the table from me, you had to cross close by the guard.

"Y'all get out from that corner. Don't need to be there anyway," the guard said to them.

An hour later, the shifts changed and Ms. Blue walked in to relieve the other guard. Ms. Blue and I would converse on nights that I couldn't sleep. She was cool and enjoyed my company as much as I enjoyed hers. She'd make everyone else rack up when it was time for lights-out, and I would be the only one left at the table with her. Sometimes she'd let Danielle stay up too, but mainly it was only Megan and I who sat around with her on the nights she worked.

"I brought the snacks and candy y'all asked for," she said as she set her clear backpack down on the table. She hands me the sour punch straws and pretzels I'd asked for two nights ago. From observing the shifts, I'd figured out that they followed a schedule of three days on, two days off. Ms. Blue was a stud with a girlfriend at home, but she'd bring me anything I asked for if I flirted with her. Even when she was stationed in a different pod, she would still bring our goodies, and we'd sneak out of Foxtrot to find her.

If a yellow badge happened to walk in while we were sitting in the day room with her after hours, we'd just lie. "Flint, why are you out of your bunk?" one of them would fuss, and I'd come up with some random excuse: "I was asking Ms. Blue if she had an extra rat trap to put by my bunk." It was easy to convince them. And once the shift change came back around, which was right before breakfast chow, I'd crawl back into my bunk.

"Everybody wake up," the new shift guard yelled as she walked in.

Oh lord, here she goes. Must've had a bad morning already. Ms. Donald was the daytime guard today. She was a very loud woman, young, dark-skinned, with her hair and face usually fixed up. This morning, she walked in with an attitude. She made everyone wake up just because she wasn't in a good mood. I pulled the covers over my head and turned over in my bunk. I never took Ms. Donald seriously, because she was another guard I would stay up and joke with all night. But she was the type of guard who would switch on you in a heartbeat. One minute, she's laughing and joking, and the next she's telling you to leave her alone, or telling everyone to shut up because she has a headache.

"You're trying to get a ten by ten unit with forty bitches to quiet down?" I asked her. "You'd better start taking the night shifts, then," I laughed.

Ms. Donald batted her long, fake eyelashes as she rolled her eyes. "Yes, it's possible for these women to shut the fuck up!"

Nobody but the new inmates or the older ones would listen. Ms. Donald and my relationship was one nobody else understood, because we would sound like we were arguing but we were really joking, except on the days when I could tell she was in a more serious mood.

I'd leave her alone on those days. Once, I tried to convince her to bring me things from the outside world, but she was one of those "I don't want to lose my job" guards. Guards were either eager to help, at least if they liked you, or else too afraid to get caught.

"You scary as fuck, I just wanted some gummy worms," I teased her. I could see in her face that she wanted to say yes, but the fear in her eyes said the opposite. You could always tell what kind of mood she was in by her appearance. On good days, she would be completely fixed up, with a new wig, eyelashes, lip gloss, makeup, and eyebrows arched. Bad days, she would come in with a hair bonnet, no makeup, and looking she'd arrived straight from out of her bed.

There was one other guard I would associate with, but only for her food. She was a big black woman who could barely fit in the door, and she brought two lunches every day. She knew how to tell an inmate no very quickly, but I'd go and talk to her while nobody was paying attention to her or her food.

"Nobody needs to ask for my food. The answer is NO," she would announce as she walked in with a big to-go box that smelled like mashed potatoes, gravy, and greasy meat. After she had to turn down three or four inmates anyway, I'd wait until I saw her slowing down and walk up to her.

"You know you got other food. Leave me a piece of that pork chop when you're done, and I'll go throw it away." I stood to one side of her and winked.

She rolled her eyes and grinned. "You think you're slick, huh?" She looked around and then nodded.

I grinned at her, proud of my accomplishment, and walked off to watch for her signal from a distance. As soon as she raised her hand to me, I got up, grabbed her plate, and walked outside. As soon as the door closed behind me, I opened the box to see a corner of mashed potatoes and half a fried pork chop. I sat down on the bench between two pods and finished the food while looking out for guards and nosy inmates, then I threw the plate in the big garbage can next to the door. I walked back inside and thanked her with my eyes. I only spoke to her when she brought food, but my innocent face was very persuasive.

I'm not exaggerating when I say this woman always had food on her. The days that she guarded the walkway, I knew she always had some kind of candy in her pockets. I'd pass her and say "What's up? They got you all in the sun today, huh?"

"Yeah, they know I hate standing out here all day."

"Go ahead and give me the yellow Starbursts you have in those pockets. I know you hate the yellow ones," I'd joke, and put my hand out.

She would look around, and roll her eyes, and finally count out three yellow Starbursts into my hand. "Better not tell anyone."

"Never. You're MY plug, nobody else's." I laughed and walked away before anyone saw us.

The next day, they called for yard around 1 p.m., after two days without yard. I rushed out of the barracks to meet up with Amy. As I passed Michigan, I heard Megan call after me.

"Cedes, where you headed? Let me find out you're looking for Amy." She batted her eyes at me, and I smiled and shoved her.

"Come on, now. She's just a cool chick," I laughed.

"Uh-huh. A cool girl with a pretty face and a fat ass that everyone trying to get a piece of. But from what I'm hearing, she's only wanting your ass," she laughed too, but I hadn't realized how Amy was feeling about me. And I did notice a lot of inmates always trying to talk to her, even though she really shut them down. I'd never known why, and now Megan was pitching me ideas about the reason.

"There goes your girl now!" She pushed me the way Amy was walking.

I looked back at Megan with a mischievous smile and then walked toward Amy. When she spotted me, she ran up with excitement and hugged me.

"Someone missing me?" I flirtatiously pushed her back.

"I do miss you. I have a letter for you, but you can't read it until you're in your pod," she told me, all nervous.

"Damn, must be breaking up with me already!" I laughed. She chuckled a little but still seemed uneasy.

"Wanna hit the track with me?" I asked, and started heading to the little trail the inmates had made with their walks.

I loved our little track walks. We talked about literally everything, especially the things we were ready to do when we got out.

"I have a year here. You have like six more months, and you're out. I will miss the shit out of you," I confided. "But I'm going to cherish the little time I get to keep my friend."

"Then let's just focus on the six months that you have me for." She smiled and looked me in the eye. Those eyes made me lose my train of thought every time I got lost in them. And she knew that they were her natural weapon.

"Yard over, rack up!" the guards yelled.

The inmates started to scatter very slowly. The longer they waited to give us yard time, the longer it took them to get us back in the pods. After being cooped up with so many women and so little sunlight, yard time was like recess at an elementary school. As usual, Amy and I took our precious time to get to where we weren't going.

"You need to write yourself out of the barracks," she told me. "That's how I moved so fast. I wrote the warden about a thousand letters saying how I was having problems with some inmates, and how I was scared for my life, blah, blah, blah."

"How do I write him, and where do I send it?" I asked.

"I've already been dropping off letters from you to the warden," she laughed. "You're the only one from the ship that hasn't moved. I'll grab you some more papers from the library to fill out for the warden."

I was relieved to hear that Amy was helping me get out of the barracks, because it was just so boring being alone even with forty women around you. We walked around the compound until we saw more guards than inmates. The guards were still trying to get everyone to rack up, since it was almost shift change. I walked Amy to her unit as she continued to explain how to get moved. She told me that she also had her whole family calling the warden and telling them how she would feel more comfortable in the compound, where she'd have only one other person in her cell.

After dropping her off, I went to Foxtrot and walked straight to the phones.

"Dad, I need a huge favor that would help both of us out," I said, in panic and excitement.

"What's that?" he asked. I loved how he never had a problem with helping me from inside.

"Could you call the warden and convince him to move me? Because I'm about ready to fight every women in this pod. In the compound, I would have my own cell and only one cellmate. All the other people who were shipped in my van have already been housed back there," I complained.

"Of course. I'll give him a call, and if he won't cooperate I'll call the lawyer," he assured me. I swear, I wouldn't know what to do without my dad.

"Thank you, I love you. Call you later," I said, hanging up. Then I remembered the dike kite that Amy gave me, so I headed to my bunk to read it.

"What's up, Cedes? I'm taking a chance here, but you've been putting the biggest smile on my face lately, and even with my old joce leaving, it's not a rebound type of thing. Like, I found you attractive since 101, but you were with Jaylon, and Vanessa was on your dick too.

And then we both ended up back in the parish and housed in the same dorm again, except that time I had a girlfriend and you were always saying how you weren't going to fuck over Diamond again. So I don't know if you're feeling the same way as I am, but it's just some kind of spark that tingles my body every time I hug you. You don't have to respond if you don't feel the same way, and I'll just leave it at our friendship. Unless I just ruined it, lol. Well, I hope to see you soon. – Amy."

My smile damn near touched my ears. It was crazy, because I was starting to feel the same way. I'd noticed myself getting excited to see Amy, and to violate just to see her, and she would violate to see me. Everyone already thought we should be together. I guessed it was time to give in. I started to write a letter back explaining that I felt the same, but then I balled it up and started over.

"Meet me at church tonight so we can talk in person. —Cedes"

After finishing the letter right on time for last chow, I stuffed it in my sock and headed out. As I was walking to the chow line to meet Danielle, I looked to see which yellow badge was clocked in, and it was one of the meanest ones, so I knew I couldn't violate today and give Amy her dike kite. When chow was over for the barracks, I saw the compound walking out, so I turned around and walked out of the gate to the barracks to see if I could find Amy that way and give her the kite, but the guards had already locked the barracks down. I stayed by the locked gate that was closest to the dining hall line. The guards were looking around to make sure that no barrack inmates were on the walkway, so I ducked and hid until I saw Amy on her way to the dining hall. It wasn't but ten minutes passing until I saw Amy walking towards the dining hall.

"What are you doing? The guards are out looking to make sure the barracks are racked up," she said with concern.

"I have your letter," I said with a smile. She turned red and smiled harder than I was. I slid the letter through the gate and turned to run toward the barracks.

When I reached Foxtrot, the guard was waiting at the door, hands on her hips. "Where were you?"

"I got lost," I laughed, and squeezed past her into the pod. It was Thursday, so I knew there was church tonight. I made sure that I was in line for church, since the strict yellow badge was in charge and she only allowed five women from each pod, including those in the compound.

Chapter 14. Time's Up

The yellow badge entered Foxtrot and called for the five inmates who were going to church. She guided us to the lines of inmates from the other pods in the barracks and then made us walk in a straight line all the way to the classroom. I saw the other yellow badges making the groups from the compound walk in straight lines too. They let the barracks in first, which meant we could grab chairs instead of the floor.

I found a seat against the back wall and put my leg on the chair next to me to save it for Amy. I looked around, and the other inmates with girlfriends from the compound were saving seats too. I watched the door as the compound inmates entered, and as soon as I saw Amy I stood up and waved. She spotted me and made her way over. The room was packed, and most of the chairs were already taken. She sat in the one I'd saved. She had fixed her hair and put a little makeup on, and she glowed next to me with that gorgeous smile of hers. We whispered and talked through the entire program.

"I do like you back, but I also cherish our friendship," I told her. "We've been rocking since the second lockup in the parish. But it's crazy, because I do find you very attractive, but I have a girlfriend at home."

"Yeah, I heard how your girl has been with other people on the outside," she said, rolling her eyes. *Damn, word gets around too quick. Fucking ear hustlers.* She got me on that one.

"You deserve better than that," she said, looking up at me with sad eyes.

After we talked about how we felt, as if we were falling for each other, the speaker finished and brought the church program to an end. As we left the classroom in a line and they gave us cookies at the door, I followed Amy to her pod. I saw all the couples just walking around the walkways before being forced to go back to their own pods.

Halfway down the walk to Kansas, Amy turned around and gave me a hug, and as we let it linger, we both just naturally leaned in for a kiss. Her eyes were closed, feeling the same spark I felt, and then she opened them softly and batted them at me with the prettiest smile. Then, like a shy little schoolgirl, she turned and walked off, looking back at me and blushing.

I turned around to walk to the barracks with a smile as wide as hers. I floated into the pod like I was walking on cloud nine and just lay in my bunk smiling. I fell asleep the same way.

The next morning, the guard woke me up around 9 a.m.

"The warden needs to speak to you. Go meet him at the front gate," she ordered.

I threw on my yellows and walked out of the pod.

At the front gate, a white man in a tuxedo was standing beside a yellow badge. I walked up to them and gave my name.

"Hello, Cedes. I received a called from your dad. He sounded very concerned about you still being in the back with forty women and suggested that you should be moved to the compound."

"Yes, sir." I gave him my sob story. "Some women are starting to harass me, and I'm just scared for my life. I'd feel more safe in a two-man cell."

"Well, your dad's a very nice guy, and I can tell he's really worried about you. So which unit would you like to be placed in?" he asked.

"Kansas," I answered a little too quickly.

"Well, go pack your things. And here—I'm sending the moving sheet with you, since it was unscheduled for your accommodations," he laughed.

"Thank you so much, Warden." I grabbed the sheet of paper and ran to the barracks. Before entering the pod, I read my name and also Misha's name. She was being moved to Louisiana. *Thank god, she wasn't going to be nowhere near me,* I thought to myself. I was too excited to get out of Foxtrot and closer to Amy. I read the the location I was moving to next to my name on the moving sheet. Kansas-A. Amy was in Kansas-B, but I wasn't complaining, because I wouldn't have to violate to be with her for chow. I could actually walk with her without looking over my shoulder for a yellow badge.

Inside Foxtrot, I went straight to my bunk.

Danielle walked up to me. "You're moving? You're leaving me too!" She got all sad in her voice.

"You need to get out of the barracks, Danielle. Write yourself out!"

I finished packing in no time and walked out of the pod, waving bye to the other inmates. Then I made my long way to the compound, ready to surprise Amy when I walked in. I passed a guard and she smiled. "Looks like someone got moved to where her girlfriend is."

I just grinned back at her as I power-walked with all my things in my hands. Then I got to the Kansas door and rang the bell for them to open the door, then I walked in and told the guards I was in KS-A.

My pod was next door to KS-B and opposite of KS-C and KS-D. I could see people in Kansas B already running to tell Amy that I'd been moved in. She appeared at the window, asking how it had happened so fast.

I walked into my pod and saw showers to the left, phones on the wall across from them, and if I looked across from the right side of the pod door, I could see the showers in Kansas B. Next to the phones were windows where you could see B pod, the closest one. C and D pods were on the other side of the tower. You could still see them, but with A and B you could literally go to the window and see each other clearly enough for window talking. There were upstairs and downstairs areas in all the pods. Both Amy and I had cells on the bottom floors.

"Damn, you're fine as fuck. Which cell are you in?" some random black woman asked as soon as I took five steps into the room.

"Aye! My dawg, Cedes!" Red ran up and dapped me up. Then she introduced me to her little girlfriend, who was in the same pod.

"Damn, I missed your ass," I laughed, and punched her.

"Same, bro. I hear you're with Amy now, huh? She got so much finer since the parish. That prison food treating her ass right," she said, and we both laughed. "I just got out of the hole last night." Red didn't go into detail about the hole, so I didn't ask.

I met my new cellmate, a thirty-year-old white lady who seemed to sleep most of the time, and then it was time for lunch chow. My bunkie didn't eat lunch, so she didn't get up.

I stood in line at the pod door and saw Amy waiting for me through the windows. As soon as they popped our door open, we all scattered out. They had to close the A-pod door before opening the others. The only time we were all released at once was when we had a guard who wasn't lazy and would actually open all doors with her own set of keys. But I waited for Amy to get let out, and we walked to chow together.

"This is crazy! Now I can see you whenever I want," she said, grabbing my arm.

We definitely looked like a couple now. We would finish chow and strolled the walkways about fifteen times just to be together like the other couples before the night ended. Sometimes we would even walk out during pill calls and stand in the pharmacy line, knowing we had no prescriptions. As soon as we reached the front of the line, we'd turn around and go to the back again. We noticed a lot of other couples doing the same thing.

One night, we walked straight back to Kansas

after chow because the strict yellow badge was on night duty. We gave each other a hug and kiss before separating. Amy window-talked to me inside, saying she was about to shower. She gave me eyes like she wanted me to watch. So I called my sister from the phone on the bench that gave me the best view of the showers next door. As I told my sister how different the compound was from the barracks, I watched Amy's naked body and forgot I was even on the phone.

"Helloooo?" I heard from the line.

I was out of words. Amy was as skinny as a twig when I first met her in the parish, but going to rehab and coming back to the parish and then to prison, her body had taken that jail food and put it in all the right places. She'd been voted sexiest white-girl body in the prison. She had me mesmerized, and she knew exactly what she was doing—she basically giving me a strip-tease performance.

I told my sister I'd call her back. I couldn't concentrate at all. I could see Amy's perfectly round titties, slim waist, wide hips, and perfectly shaved vagina, and when she turned around, there was her round ass that looked like two big beach balls taped side by side.

I finally had to walk away from the window. I could see Amy laughing at me for not being able to handle the teasing. I wished I could be in the dorm with her.

Looking around the dorm from a table in the day room, I saw locked doors leading to the B pod on both floors. I started to wonder and think. But I had to see what they were used for first. I went to my bunk to fix my bed and then got ready for a shower. As I walked to the showers, I had about three women following me with no clothes in hand, which made me suspect they were just shower stalking. As I undressed, I looked out the window and saw Amy taking a seat on the bench to have herself a show from me. I could see her face turn to anger as she watched the other women surround me.

"You're so sexy," one told me.

"My girl is right on the other side of that window." Even though we'd never made it official, I said it to make the other women leave me alone. They looked across.

"Damn, that fine-ass white girl's for you?"

I grinned and stepped into the shower to wash off.

After I finished drying and putting on my nightclothes, the pod door popped open. "Cedes, come see." Ms. Donald waved me over.

I followed her, and she escorted me into of the tower. I saw Amy go to her window to see what was going on. I'd never been in the tower, or even seen any other inmates inside.

"Tell them your ethnicity," she told me, in front of two other guards.

"I'm black and Asian," I answered for the fiftieth time since being here. When they did head counts, they used race. The blacks and the whites, and since I'm mainly Asian, that was the ethnicity I went by.

"Yeah, this one always messes my count up. I always mark her down as white because she looks white." Ms. Donald laughed to the other guards.

"I ain't messed shit up. We're always arguing because you want to mark me down as white, when I try to correct you that I am black. Not my fault you're colorblind." That made the other guards laugh.

The doorbell buzzed, meaning someone was at the pod door.

"Shit, it's a yellow badge," Ms. Donald said. You couldn't pop open the outside door if any of the unit's doors were open. A guard told me to close the door, and I unthinkingly closed myself inside the tower. The yellow badge walked in and walked right up to the tower.

"What the fuck is an inmate doing in the tower with doors closed?"

I tried to sneak past the yellow badge and back to my dorm, and they popped the pod A open for me, but I heard the yellow badge yell after me, "Next time I catch you in the tower, I will put you on bed confinement!"

I saw Amy in the window so I walked over. She signs me, "What happened?" and I signed back that Ms. Donald took me out to ask for my ethnicity, and then I shrugged.

I saw Amy getting mad. "They better hop off your dick before I say something!"

"You ain't goin' do shit," I joked, and it make her smile. I turned back to the pod when I heard the door pop.

"Tyra McKinsey!"

I turned toward Red's cell and saw her walk out to see what was wanted. The yellow badge took her outside to talk to her, and she walked back in dancing and jumping around. She came up to me and said, "I got accepted into work release! I'm being shipped out in the morning!"

I gave her a hug and congratulated her. I was happy to see her go, but sad that I'd finally been placed with her and she was already leaving.

Red went to her cell and told her girlfriend the news. She wasn't too happy about it either. Tears were running down her cheeks.

"You don't have much longer after me. I'll see you on the outside," Red told her girlfriend.

After she finished packing, she came to my cell with a big, gray storage container. "Here. This is way bigger and better than that duffle bag," she said, setting the container on the floor. "They're going to ship me around two in the morning."

"Get out of here and get back on your feet, Red. You got this," I dapped her up and then gave her a big hug.

After that, I sat down with Red and her girlfriend to play spades until lights-out. Then the pod door popped open, and a guard walked in with a pencil and pad. I assumed she was doing count. She made us all stop what we were doing and go to our cells for a second. As she made her rounds and approached the door that led to pod A, I watched closely. She unlocked the door and closed it behind her. I rolled my eyes. I'd have to wait until she forgot to close it before I could try out my plan.

After the guard counted all four pods, she let us out of the cells, and we got back to our spades table. When lights-out came, I went to the window and blew

Amy kisses. She told me to go to the door that separated the pods. I went to the door, and from the other side I heard Amy saying she wished she could hug me and kiss me. I told her I wished the same. Then a piece of paper slid through the gap under the door. I took the letter, and we told each other goodnight.

I heard a bang on my cell door and my name being called around one in the morning.

"Cedes, I'm getting out of this bitch. I'll see you soon, bro!" Red yelled.

"Be good out there! I'll find you," I yelled back.

Before I could fall asleep again, it was morning chow, but I stayed in my cell. Once everyone returned to their cells to go back to sleep. I watched the guard do her morning count, unlocking the cells one by one with her keys as she did. When she went through the door to the other pod, she didn't close it all the way.

I peeked out of my cell and saw nobody in the day room. I grabbed a piece of cardboard that I'd folded up and left lying around, apparently out of boredom, and headed up to the half-closed door. Looking around quietly, I opened the door just enough to see the hole the latch would fit into, and I stuffed the cardboard inside. It filled the hole about two-thirds of the way. I shifted the door back to where it had been and walked back to my cell and went to sleep.

When I woke up for lunch chow, I saw that the pod door was closed tightly. I was eager to see whether my plan would work, but I waited for Amy. As we walked to chow together, I had the biggest smile on my face.

"You're extra happy," she smiled back at me.

"I have a little plan I want to try out when we get back," I told her.

"Oh god, you're always up to something." She gave a nervous laugh.

After eating, and taking our daily laps around the compound until we were the only ones being rushed back to our pods, I leaned against the tower wall where the guards in the tower couldn't see me. When they popped open the B pod, I crawled in as fast as I could. I pulled my hoodie up and walked to Amy's cell.

"Oh my god, how are you going to get out of here?" She started to panic.

I walked her to the pod door that separated us. Since it was under the staircase, the guards couldn't see into the area.

"Give me your ID." I put my hand out. She gave it to me, looking confused as hell. I slipped the ID into the little space between the door and the frame, then I slid it down quickly and heard a *click*. I pulled the door open, and Amy's mouth dropped.

"You fucked up. Now we can't let people see this, or they'll blow our spot," she said.

"I know. So we can only use it for emergencies."

"All my emergencies are needing you in here with me." She gave me those puppies eyes I couldn't resist. Still, it was too risky to open the door during the day, with most of the inmates being in the day room where they could see it.

"I'll come over tonight, depending on the night shift guards. If the easy guards are working, I'll come visit you," I assured her.

She smiled and gave me a big kiss and hug, and I walked through the door to my pod, shutting it behind me. I saw a few eyes staring at me in awe, but I walked straight to my cell and waited for dinner.

When chow was called, I saw that the nice guard was clocked in. The guard went door to door, unlocking them to let us all out at the same time. Amy and I walked to chow together, damn near holding hands with how close we were walking. I'd been in the compound almost a week now, and it had been the best week of being incarcerated. We would violate to go to the library, violate to go to classes we weren't even taking, and even violate while bringing laundry to the washing room.

After chow, we hugged and kissed each other, knowing that once we got into our pods, we'd sit right in the windows to talk to each other anyway. There would be about three other couples doing the same, just sitting there all day window talking. I was one of them now.

After the last count before lights-out, I got ready to pop the door and sneak in to see Amy. We went to the window first to make sure the coast was clear, and Amy pointed to the door. I met her there.

"These guards are easy," she whispered. "You're free to come over."

I grabbed my ID and returned to pop the door. Luckily, Amy's cell was right next to it. I went straight in and lay on her bunk like it was mine. She lay beside me, and I held her and started to rub her body. I could feel her heat up as I touched her. I let my hands wander around her body and then slid them into her pants and felt how wet she was just from my touch. I looked in her eyes, feeling her getting wetter and wetter. I bit her neck, and she moaned.

"*Whoop, whoop!* That ass *fat!*" We heard the code for a guard walking in.

I jumped up and looked out the little window in the cell door. The guard was already in the day room. There was no way I could sneak past her to the door. I had to sit it out. Amy was a talker too, so she also had guards who were friends with her and would come into the dorm just to visit and chat. I saw the guard walking our way.

"She's coming here," I said, hiding my panic. Amy's eyes had terror in them. This was it, we were caught.

The guard opened the door. "Amy! What you doing in your cell? You normally out in the window with your—oh." She stopped when she saw me. "What the hell?"

I stood up. "What's good, miss Ma'am. Lovely night to hop pods, am I right?" I snuck past the guard, popped the side door open, and walked back into A pod. Then I made my way to the phones to call Diamond. I hadn't talked to her since I moved to Kansas.

"Hello?"

"What's up, baby? I miss you. Are you doing okay out there?" I asked her.

"Yeah, everything is okay, I guess." She sounded sad and dry.

"Anything you want to tell me?"

"No, I'm just depressed," she complained.

Like I'm not fighting a horrible depression in here. Everyday was a struggle not to just rage and throw tantrums.

I told Diamond goodnight and hung up, and then scooted over to the window to look through to B pod. Amy was already waiting for me. We started window talking.

"Did you get in trouble? What did the guard say?" I signed.

"She didn't say nothing, except that you were sexy, and that we were lucky it was just her that caught us."

I laughed.

The next day, I was woken in my cell by Ms. Donald. It felt like about 9 a.m. She told me to throw on my yellows and come with her. Sleepy-eyed, I pulled my clothes on as I walked behind her.

"What's going on?"

"I'm not sure, but it might be good," she told me. "So you and Amy, huh?" She rolled her eyes.

"Uh-huh, I knew you liked me. Always stunting and never bringing me any candy," I joked back.

"Nobody hating on y'all's lesbian activities." She rolled her eyes again with those long, fake eyelashes.

"Keep rolling those eyes, them lashes gonna fall out with them," I laughed at her. She playfully shoved me off the walkway.

When we reached the warden's office, she held the door open for me. I saw one chair in front of the warden's desk.

"Cedes, how is Kansas treating you?"

"Better than the barracks, Warden. Thank you for the move."

"Well, don't get too comfortable. Your lawyer called, and apparently your co-defendant, the one who was shot fled after being released from the hospital. They picked her up in California during a traffic stop. Found drugs, guns, and a lot more. So your lawyer contacted the judge, and explained how you had nothing to do with that the entire time. The judge agreed to let you out next week—only because we need a little time get all the release papers situated. And well . . . that is all, ma'am," the warden finished.

The corners of my mouth must have reached my ears. I was as happy as a blind man getting a fresh set of eyes. The walk back to the compound was long. I kept thinking about how happy I was to get out, but I felt bad that I was leaving Amy behind. She was supposed to get out before me.

I got to the pod and decided not to tell her just yet. The church was hosting a Christmas festival for us under the pavilion the Friday before I would be released.

I went straight to the window, seeing Amy already waiting for me with concern on her face. I signed that everything was okay, and that the warden wanted to know how I was liking the compound. Amy smiled and told me she couldn't wait for the Christmas party.

The day of the party, I had my yellows all nice and crispy. The guards started popping open the doors to all the pods. As I waited for Amy by her pod's door, I noticed there were no guards in the tower. I walked in pod B and straight to Amy's cell and closed the door behind me.

"Oh shit," she said as she turned around, half-dressed.

"You might as well just take it off," I told her, eyeing her suggestively.

"We have to go to the party," she said, biting her lip.

"This won't take but one minute."

"It definitely will not take me only one minute," she said sternly.

"Is that a challenge?" I pushed her onto her bunk and took her pants off.

I kissed her belly all the way down to her hips, feeling her jump from the tingling sensations I was sending through her. Then I slid my tongue down to her pussy lips, and I ran into a ring. *She has her clit pierced!* That was sexy as hell. Even more turned on, I wrapped my lips around her clit and the ring. She moaned and grabbed my hair as I licked and sucked on her clit. She pulled my hair tighter, and in a matter of seconds I felt her climaxing. Her legs wouldn't stop shaking the whole time. I heard a noise and got a little paranoid, but it was nothing. I looked back at her and saw her legs still shaking from her orgasm. I picked her pants up and handed them to her.

"See? A minute. Forty-five seconds, really, but I'll give you the minute."

She shoved me playfully. "Why'd you do that shit? That was like the best ever."

After she dressed, she pulled me out the dorm to

meet everyone under the pavilion. She couldn't hold her smile back, making it obvious what had just gone down. I started feeling bad about leaving her again, but I was ready to get out of there.

The little Christmas party was fun for prison activities, but we really went there for the free "real food." They had nachos with chili and cheese, candied popcorn, and all kinds of candy that weren't offered on the commissary. We stayed through the whole event, and when it was over, the guards had to try their hardest to rack everyone up. Like every other couple, Amy and I took our time getting back to the pods. But once the yellow badges came out and everyone scattered, we followed suit and went to our own pods.

I went to the phones in Kansas-A and called Diamond to tell her the good news.

"Hello?"

"Baby . . . you can come pick me up tomorrow! They found Stacey, and they're releasing me!" I tried to not sound too eager.

There was just silence for a moment.

"Are you too happy to talk?" I asked her.

"Are you sure you want me to pick you up," she said.

"I had no doubts about you picking me up, but now I do. What's wrong?"

"I mean, we haven't even been talking lately, and when we do we just argue. I just thought that maybe you'd want your dad to pick you up," she explained.

That stung. In my mind, I was ready to get out and be with her regardless of what she was doing out in the real world.

"Hello? Cedes?" she called.

I had nothing more to say. My feelings being hurt by her response, I just hung up. I called my dad and told him what I'd told Diamond.

"Whattttt!? I will be there as soon as the gates open, baby," he screamed in my ear.

I couldn't even be as excited anymore, knowing the first face I wanted to see was my girlfriend's. If I even had a girlfriend anymore.

I could barely sleep that night, looking through all the letters and pictures I had from Diamond, and just wondering what had happened. The only thing I could think of was her meeting someone else, and there wasn't much more I could do from this side of the walls. I'd even sent her flowers from prison. I just didn't understand.

When morning chow came around, Ms. Donald came to my cell and told me to follow her.

"Your ride is here. Let's get you checked out."

She popped open the pod door, and I saw Amy at her window, waving to me with her sad eyes. She yelled through the door, "Donald, just let me out real quick to hug her bye!"

Rolling her eyes under her fake lashes, she popped the door open, and Amy rushed out to hug me. She felt like she didn't want to let go. Eventually Ms. Donald made her go back into her pod, and she walked me to the front entrance. In the classroom where we'd received our yellows, I put the clothes I'd arrived in back on my body, and then the guard walked me through the open gate to freedom. As I took a few steps toward the parking lot, I heard my name.

"Cedes!"

I saw my dad and ran to him.

"You hungry for cooked food?" he asked me.

"More than you could imagine." I laughed. As we drove away, I let out a sigh of relief while looking back at the gated facility. Almost six months in the parish jail, and three in prison. I'd never look back at that place again.

To be continued...

www.ingramcontent.com/pod-product-compliance
Lightning Source LLC
Chambersburg PA
CBHW021156160726
47994CB00001B/242